Granny's Message

By

Debbie Williams

Preface

"Does God allow people who have passed away to communicate with those of us who are still alive? Does love carry through to the other side?" These are questions that have plagued mankind for thousands of years. This novel is a work of complete fiction, but it does deal with the question of messages from the other side. I have had a few experiences in my life which would lead me to believe that it is possible. However, what I do know for certain is that believers are going to believe, and the skeptics will find ways to explain away anything. I guess that we all must decide for ourselves.

Prologue

Jamie Barnes sat in the office of the Valene School District superintendent's office. While she waited for John Newsome to finish reading her resume, she focused on not swiveling her chair due to her anxiety. After a short amount of time, he looked up and smiled.

"Your references are impressive," he told her.

"Thank you," she answered.

"I am a little curious about something," he continued.

"What is that?" Jamie asked.

"I see that you are from Grove City, Ohio. You did some extensive substitute teaching there for several years and you apparently made quite an impression on their administrators. However, Valene, Wisconsin is quite a distance from central Ohio. I was just wondering why you are applying to a district so far away from your home. Was there some problem as to why you were never hired full time in that area?"

Jamie smiled. She wasn't unprepared for this question. "My father was very ill during that time, and I needed to help my mother care for him. I was on the substitute list for a couple of districts near my home. As a substitute teacher I was able to control what days that I worked so that I could be available to take my father to appointments and help my mother when needed. He passed away last January, and then my mother moved to Florida right after his death, so I decided that it was time for a change in my life. There weren't many jobs available for the upcoming school year in the districts where I had worked, so I expanded my search and I happened to see that you were looking for a second and third grade teacher, so I decided to take a chance and apply for the jobs."

The man appeared to consider her words for a moment, and then finally spoke. "I'm very sorry about your father. My wife and I went through the same thing a couple of years ago with her mother. I understand how difficult that situation can be."

"Thank you," she said to him.

"Well, Miss Barnes," he then continued. "We had a student teacher in our building last fall who is hoping to take the third-grade position. However, I have yet to come across a suitable candidate to complete the 2nd grade staff...until today. The elementary principal and the staff committee that interviewed you yesterday were also impressed by you. I would like to submit your name to the school board for approval next week, if you are truly interested in making the move here."

Jamie's heart soared. Since she had arrived in the small town of Valene, Wisconsin, she had felt that this was a place that she would be happy living in. The last few years of her life had been a struggle to live through, but suddenly she had a

5

feeling that things were about to change...for the
better.

Chapter One

The sky was just turning a pale pink when Jamie turned onto I-270 which was the bypass interstate around Columbus. From there she would be able to connect to I-70 and head toward Indianapolis. According to Google Maps, she should arrive in that city by mid-morning.

Just about a month earlier she had received a phone call from John Newsome giving her the good news that she had been hired as a second-grade teacher in the Valene School District. She would be assigned to Riley Elementary, which was a small school located in the town of Riley not far from Valene. As she understood, Riley was a very rural community. Both Riley and Valene were located within fifty miles of Madison, Wisconsin.

John Newsome had surprised her with some other interesting news. He and his wife, Carol, owned a small house just outside of Riley that was available for rent. Apparently, Riley did not have a lot to offer in the line of apartment rentals, other than one low-income complex. Beyond that, she probably would have to look at some rentals in Valene, which was a good fifteen-mile drive. The house which he owned was actually just outside of Riley and only a five-minute drive from the school.

The following week, Jamie had flown to Madison, and rented a car to make the drive to Valene. She had met with John Newsome and signed her contract. Then he and his wife drove her to the rental house.

Jamie was pleased with what she saw. The small white bungalow was perfect. It was situated on a side road just about a half of a mile off a main highway. The house was close enough for easy access to town, but far enough away to enjoy some peace and quiet.

Inside the home, there was a nice sized living room with a fireplace and a mantle. John apologized for the fact that the fireplace was not usable, but he assured her that the flu was sealed up tightly to keep the heat in and unwelcome animals out. The room contained a comfortable looking sofa and a worn looking recliner. Behind the living room there was a small kitchen and dining area. The kitchen was surprisingly updated with a flat top stove and a stainless-steel refrigerator with French doors and a freezer on the bottom. There was also a new-looking dishwasher. In the dining area there was a small table and four chairs. Carol explained that the home had belonged to her grandmother who was now in an assisted living home. Apparently, right after her grandmother had moved out, there had been a leak under the sink and the kitchen had been flooded. It was several days before the problem was discovered, and the appliances had all been shorted out and the floor was ruined, so everything in the kitchen had to be replaced. One thing that Jamie was happy to see was a closet that contained a stackable washer and dryer. The idea of going to a laundromat every week was not appealing.

Carol's mother had assumed the responsibility of taking care of the house and she had rented it to the 2nd grade teacher that Jamie was replacing. After the death of Carol's mother, the Newsome's had taken over as landlords of the house. The 2nd grade teacher had gotten married during the previous year. She had remained in the house until the school year was finished, and then she moved with her husband to Chicago.

Down the hall there was a bedroom with a metal bed frame with no mattress and a small dresser. The Newsomes told her that the previous tenant had bought a new mattress and that she had taken it with her when she left. There was also a double closet. The only bathroom in the house was located right next to the bedroom. There was one more small room that Jamie thought would make a nice place to do her schoolwork and to place her sewing machine and Cricut so that she could continue to do the crafts that she loved.

After they had looked the house over, the three of them sat at the table and discussed rent and lease options. Jamie agreed to their terms and signed a one-year lease of the house. The next day she flew back to Ohio and began to make preparations for the move. It was only the middle of June, but her mother's house had been sold and she needed to be out by the 1st of July.

The next two weeks were a whirlwind of getting electric, cable, water, and internet arranged for her new home. She also managed to apply for a Wisconsin teaching certificate which was promised to be valid by the 1st week of school.

Her biggest problem was arranging to move her personal items to Wisconsin. A good teaching friend, Pam, and her husband, Jeff, volunteered to help by Jeff driving a small U-Haul truck while the two women followed in Pam's car. Jamie's car had a lot of miles on it, so she decided to sell it before the move. At a local dealership, she arranged to lease a new SUV which she would pick up in Madison. The plan was for the couple to help her unload the truck, return the rental, and then drive home the following day.

Unfortunately, Pam had to have an emergency appendectomy just before the scheduled move. Jamie insisted that if she had help loading the truck, she could manage to drive it by herself to her new home. During a phone call to Carol Newsome, she was happy to learn that Carol would send her sons to help unload the truck if needed. There weren't many heavy items in the truck. Most of the furniture in her mother's home had been moved to Florida or had been sold with the house.

About twelve-thirty in the afternoon, she exited the interstate at a small town and chose a local diner to have lunch. The restaurant wasn't busy, so she was in and out in about forty minutes. She had to park the truck in a parking lot around the corner, and as she was walking back to the lot, she happened to pass a small antique store. For some unknown reason, she stopped to look in the window. Her attention was drawn to a chair that was placed in the center of the display. Jamie had very little knowledge of antiques, but

The truck wasn't difficult to drive. It was easy to see out of it because she was sitting up high, and so far, there had not been much traffic. When mapping out her route, she carefully planned to take the outer routes around Indianapolis, Chicago, and Madison. If she did encounter heavy traffic, her plan was to go slow and stay in the right lane as much as possible.

something about the chair spoke to her. It was a sturdy looking brown, wooden, rocking chair with a cane back and curved handles. It just looked as if it were inviting her to sit down and have a relaxing rock in it.

After a moment she shrugged off the feeling, assuming that she was just tired from rising early and driving for several hours. Back in the truck, she dug into the cooler that was on her passenger seat and pulled out a Mountain Dew, hoping the caffeine would help keep her alert until she reached Chicago.

About three hours later, she arrived at the outskirts of the city. She was able to easily maneuver her way onto I-490 and then a few minutes later, she connected to interstate 90, and began the last leg of her journey. Just after she crossed the Wisconsin state line, she stopped for a quick dinner and then continued toward Madison.

Her excitement began to mount the closer she came to her destination. Originally, she had planned to stop somewhere around Madison and get a hotel room. Then she could arrive at the house early in the morning and be fresh to begin unloading, but somehow the closer she got to her new home, a different plan began to form in her mind. One of the last things that was loaded into the van was the new mattress that she had purchased. It wasn't heavy and she was almost certain that she could drag it out and slide it into the bedroom. If not, she would sleep on the sofa. The two hundred dollars that she would not be spending on a hotel room would be useful in the next few weeks in which she would be setting up housekeeping.

A couple of hours later, she pulled the truck into the driveway of the house and turned off the ignition. A sense of gratitude flooded over her for reaching her new home safely. After saying a quick prayer of thanks, she exited the truck and walked to the front door. Looking down, she spotted the rock that Carol had told her that she would place the key under. Once she had the key in her hand, she took a moment to   place it on her key ring. Then she opened the door and flipped the switch on the wall, and the room was flooded with light. Jamie stepped inside and stared at the plush couch. All thoughts of dragging the mattress inside faded away. Within an hour, she was curled up on the couch, sound asleep.

The next morning, she woke up around eight o'clock. After taking a moment to remember where she was, she sat up and looked around. She had pulled the curtains closed just before she had gone to bed the night before, but she could see that the sunlight was spilling through the top and sides of the windows. After she opened the curtains, it appeared to be a beautiful summer morning.

At that moment her stomach growled, and she realized that in her haste to make it to her new home, she had forgotten to stop to buy food. After she wandered into the kitchen and searched the cabinets and the refrigerator, she realized that she had a dilemma. The only way that she had of obtaining breakfast was to drive the loaded truck into town and get some food. Should she just look for donuts and coffee, or should she look for a grocery store? Then she remembered that her plan was to get the truck unloaded and return it to the U-Haul location in Valene today to avoid further charges. Her leased SUV was also available at the Chevy dealership at 1:00 today.

After a moment of thought, she took a very quick shower and put on clean clothes. In the town, she found a gas station that had a small grocery store with fresh hot coffee and a supply of pastries from a local bakery. Fifteen minutes later, she was back in her kitchen enjoying her breakfast. When she was finished, she called Carol and asked her if her sons were still available to help unload her truck. Fortunately, they didn't have football practice until later that day and were able to come and help.

Thirty minutes later, the two teenage boys arrived in an older model truck and Carol followed in a newer looking Buick. The boys were both good-sized young men and they told Jamie that they could handle it all themselves if she would just direct them where to put the items. Within an hour, the truck was empty, and the boys were on their way to football practice. Jamie made several attempts to pay them, but they refused to take any money, explaining that they wouldn't have to lift quite as many weights in the weight room that night.

After they left, Carol offered to follow her to the U-Haul store and take her to lunch afterwards. Her kind offer warmed Jamie's heart and she felt as if she had made her first new friend. Over lunch, she learned several interesting things. The boys that had helped unload her truck were seventeen-year-old twins who were juniors at Valene High School. John and Carol also had an older daughter who was married and lived in Green Bay.

The most interesting discussion they had was about the local school system. Carol had worked at Riley Elementary for several years as a music teacher, and John had taught biology at the high school. Eventually, he became the principal and two years later, he was hired as the district superintendent. Carol had resigned as a teacher a year later. She explained that it had put her in an awkward position at times because she was married to everyone's supervisor. Also at that time, there were several older teachers who tended to be quite opinionated, and she had overheard a couple of conversations where they were discussing how nice it must be to be married to the boss and being able to do whatever you wanted without having to worry about consequences. After leaving her position, she began giving private music lessons and teaching some online music theory classes for a college in Madison.

Just as she finished that particular story, the waiter brought their sandwiches. Jamie gave some thought to the part of the story about the two gossipy teachers. She had encountered some of those kinds of people over the last few years, and she generally tried to avoid them as much as possible.

"Do those older women still work at Riley?" she asked, almost afraid to hear the answer.

Carol smiled. "The two worst of them have retired. You won't have to worry about them. There is only one of the old guard left and she pretty much keeps to herself. They have tried to force her out, but she is hanging in there. She has been reassigned as a remedial reading teacher so that no child has to put up with her grumpiness for more than thirty minutes a day."

"That's sad," Jamie said.

"I know," Carol answered. "It's sad for the kids and it's sad for her. Bessie must have a lonely miserable existence, especially since the other...oh I guess I left that part out. You see, she and two of the other older teachers were like a little group. They did everything together. Dora and Brenda retired about three years ago. The plan was that

Bessie was going to retire after one more year. Well, the September after the first two retired, they took a day trip to Madison to go shopping at some flea markets. It was a school day so Bessie couldn't go. Tragically, they were both killed in a car accident on the way home. Naturally Bessie was devastated at the loss of her friends."

"I'm sure she was," Jamie answered. "That's very sad."

"Yes," Carol replied. "That is why the district has not pushed as hard as they might have to get her to retire. She has no family, and her job is probably the only reason she has to get out of bed in the morning. I think that she pushed it as far as she can though."

"Do you mean this might be her last year?" Jamie asked.

Carol nodded. "I really shouldn't say anymore."

"I understand," Jamie told her. "I'm just glad that you gave me a heads up about the situation."

"I just wanted you to understand," Carol told her as she smiled. "If you encounter her and she seems to be in a mood, just make a wide circle around her."

"Got it," Jamie answered.

A few minutes later as they were finishing their lunch, Carol looked at her watch. "Oh my. Look at the time. I have a couple of piano lessons later this afternoon. I can drop you off at the dealership to pick up your car if you would like."

"That would be fantastic," Jamie told her. "I certainly appreciate all of your kindness."

"It's not a problem," Carol replied. "We are happy to have a responsible renter in the house. I think John would be happy to just sell the place, but Grandma is still alive, and I am just not emotionally ready to do that yet. It has been a lot with Mother's passing so recently."

"I completely understand," Jamie agreed. "After my father died, my mother sold everything and took off to Florida without giving any thought to my feelings about our home or consider that I was grieving too."

Carol sighed. "I guess we all deal with things in different ways."

One week later, Jamie felt like she could finally relax. After days of unpacking and several trips to Walmart and a few to Home Depot, everything was put away and organized, and there wasn't a box in sight. Walking through the house, she felt at home. In the living room, she stopped and stared for a moment. The room was bare, and she knew why. The morning before, Carol's boys had come to do the mowing and they had loaded the old recliner onto their truck as per the conversation that she and Carol had had on the phone the night before. The chair was not only old, but it would not recline properly, so the boys were going to take it to the dump.

After a moment of contemplation, she suddenly decided to make a trip into town, although she wasn't entirely sure why. Driving down the main street, she wasn't sure what she was looking for until she suddenly saw an antique shop. Without giving it a thought, she parked her SUV and went inside the store.

For a few minutes, she wandered around aimlessly through the place. The front of the store had some nice things displayed, but the items in the back part were not very organized, but rather just placed wherever they would best fit. By the time she reached that section, she had just about decided that there was really nothing of interest in the store. Then she happened to see something stuck in a back corner. It was a wooden rocking chair that was piled with old pillows and a couple of plastic flower sets.

She walked over closer to it and soon realized that it was very similar to the chair that she had seen in the window of the antique store the day she had made the move. The only difference was that it was painted white. Looking around, Jamie noticed that the only person working in the store was a lady who was near the check-out desk, but she was completely wrapped up in a conversation on her cell phone.

Jamie walked over to the desk and waited politely for the woman to finish her conversation. A couple of minutes later, she did and then smiled at Jamie.

"Good morning. Is there something I can help you with?"

"Yes," Jamie answered. "There is a rocking chair in the back. It's covered with flowers and pillows. I am wondering if it is for sale. I might be interested in it."

The woman frowned and walked toward the back of the store while Jamie followed. When she reached the area, the woman smiled as she realized what chair that she was referring to. Then she turned back to Jamie.

"That chair was a lovely rocker until someone foolishly painted over the original wood stain." She pulled all the pillows and flowers off the chair and turned it around. "See?"

Jamie leaned down and saw what the woman was referring to. There was a place where someone had started to scrape the paint off and the original brown stain was revealed.

"Oh, that's a shame," Jamie said.

"Yes, it is," the woman answered. "It could still be a nice chair. It is in good shape, structurally." She turned it back around and gave it a push to show how well it rocked. "The paint could be scraped off with some serious elbow grease. Then it could be stained back to the original brown. Do you know anything about restoring furniture?"

Jamie shook her head. "I'm afraid I don't, but I guess I could learn. Do you have a price on the chair?"

The woman thought for a moment. She sighed and then said, "Since I have no idea how much work will be involved in restoring it, I could let you have it for twenty dollars."

Jamie thought for a moment and then sat down in the chair and began to rock. Suddenly, a sense of feeling at home came over her. Then without another thought, she said, "I'll take it."

Ten minutes later, the two of them managed to load the chair into the back of her Blazer. Jamie then asked her where the best place was to get her supplies for restoring the chair. The woman then directed her to a hardware store just a few doors down. Jamie thanked her, locked the Blazer, and walked down the street.

Inside the store, she met a very friendly gentleman working behind the counter. When she began to explain her project to him, he led her to the aisle where all those supplies were located. After she asked him several more questions, the man smiled at her and then gave her news that was a little disheartening.

"Young lady, this project sounds like it is going to take a lot of work," he began. "I get the impression that you are not very experienced with working with furniture."

At that point, her face turned slightly red. "No, I am not."

The kind man smiled at her. "Well, I think this may not be a project for a beginner, but I may be able to help you in another way. My name is Ed, and my brother, Earl, and I own this store and we run a little side business. Earl works on furniture in our back room. If you would like, you can bring the chair in here and he could give you an estimate of what he would charge you to refinish it. Is that something that you might consider?"

Jamie felt a sense of relief. "I think I might be willing to hear an estimate."

"All right," he answered. "Where is the chair now?"

"It is in the back of my Blazer, which is parked in front of the antique store," she told him.

Ed nodded and pointed to the right. "There is an alley running past here. Pull your vehicle down the alley and turn right. I will be there waiting by the back door."

"Thank you. I will," Jamie said and then hurried back down the street. As she made the short drive, she hoped this didn't turn out to be outrageously expensive because the idea of restoring the chair by herself seemed more daunting by the minute.

True to his word, Ed was waiting in the back of the store when she pulled up. He unloaded the chair for her and carried it to the backroom. After taking a moment to inspect the chair, he shook his head and spoke.

"I don't understand why people do such stupid things. This was a beautiful chair at one time."

"Do you think that it can be restored?" she asked.

"I'm sure that it can," he told her. "The question is how much work and supplies it's going to take. Earl had to run to the bank. He'll be back in a few minutes. Do you have any other errands to run?"

"I guess that I could go have some lunch," she answered. "I could come back after that."

"That will work," he said. "The special at the deli is chicken salad on a croissant today and it is amazing."

"That sounds good," Jamie answered. "Where is that?"

Ed smiled. "I thought you were new in town. It is a couple of blocks down from here. You can't miss it. It's the only restaurant in this part of town."

"Thank you," she said with a grin. "Do you always check out the specials ahead of time?"

He laughed. "No. Today is Thursday."

"I see," she told him. "Well, thank you. I think I'm going to like living here. Everyone that I have met has been very kind."

"If you don't mind me asking, what brings you to our small town?" he wanted to know.

"I have been hired as a 2nd grade teacher at the elementary school," she answered.

His face then showed a realization. "Oh, are you the young lady that is renting the Newsome house on Ranch Road?"

"Yes. I am," she replied. "I guess there are no secrets in a small town?"

Ed smiled. "John and the boys did a little sprucing up before you moved in," he told her. "They stopped in for some supplies and he told me that they had rented the house to a new teacher."

"I see," she said with a smile. "Well, I'll be back in a little while."

"Enjoy your lunch," he said as she climbed back in her Blazer and drove off.

A few minutes later, Jamie was served her chicken salad sandwich and she decided that Ed was right. It was delicious. It was a little early for the lunch rush, so there was only one other table occupied in the dining room. While she ate, Jamie found herself compelled to watch them. The man appeared to be in his late twenties or may be his early thirties, and he was dressed in blue jeans and a plaid shirt. His hair was dark brown, and he was sporting a kind of scruffy beard. There was a black cowboy hat sitting on the table, which Jamie

27

found a little unusual. Who knew that there were cowboys in Wisconsin? The woman sitting across from him was much older than him, possibly in her fifties or sixties. She was dressed in casual work clothes and her hair looked freshly styled. Jamie wondered if they were mother and son.

Whoever they were, the two of them appeared to be in a very intense conversation. Jamie couldn't hear what they were saying, but she had the impression that they were disagreeing about something. Eventually, the waitress brought their bill and the two of them stood to leave. The man put on his hat and the two of them walked toward the register. As he passed her table, the man looked at her, tipped his hat and said, "ma'am."

Jamie was a little taken back. Did he just call her *"ma'am?"*

She didn't ever remember being referred to as a *ma'am* before. It was a little unsettling. She had just turned twenty-five and she always thought of herself as a miss. Ma'am was for older women like in their thirties or older. Then she shrugged and decided that maybe it was just a country thing.

About twenty minutes later, Jamie returned to the hardware store, where Ed led her to the back room and introduced her to his brother, Earl. The two men looked very much alike, and Jamie wondered if they were twins. The chair was sitting on a table and turned so that the scraped section on the back was easier to see, especially with the very bright lights in the room.

"I can restore the chair to its original state," Earl told her. "It will take me about a week, though."

"How much will it cost?" Jamie asked hopefully.

The two men exchanged a look, and Jamie had the feeling that a silent message was exchanged between the two of them.

"I'm just curious," Ed said. "How much did Velma charge you?"

"Velma?"

"Velma is the owner of the antique store," Earl explained. "She is our cousin."

"Oh. I see," she said. "Since it needed some work, she only charged me twenty dollars."

"The chair is probably no more than fifty years old," Earl told her. "If you were to buy this in a store in a restored condition, you would likely pay between one hundred and one hundred and fifty dollars." He thought for another moment and then continued. "I will do it for a hundred dollars and then you will have one twenty in it."

Jamie didn't have to think long about that. "That sounds fair," she answered.

"Good deal," Earl said. "I will get started on it this afternoon. Leave your number with Ed and we will call you when it is finished."

Later that night, she spent some time studying herself in the mirror, trying to decide if she was really old enough to be a ma'am. Was she starting to age a little early without realizing it? After a few moments of inspecting her dark brown hair for any early strands of grey, and her eyes for any emerging crow's feet, she came to the conclusion that she was not aging prematurely. Actually, she found herself moderately attractive. Maybe she was not the blonde bombshell that her last boyfriend had cheated on her with, but she could hold her own.

To Jamie's delight, Earl finished the project on the following Wednesday and was kind enough to deliver it to her house in his truck. As soon as he left, Jamie sat in the chair and experienced the same sense of being at home that she had felt at the store. She closed her eyes and quietly rocked for a few peaceful minutes. Just as she felt herself possibly drifting off to sleep, there was a loud noise at her front door. Completely startled, she sat straight up in the chair. In the few weeks that she had lived there, no one had knocked on her door that she wasn't expecting. Then the sound repeated, and she realized that it was not a knock, but it was closer to a thump.

She decided that the wisest thing to do was go to the window and look out. When she did, she was totally surprised. What she saw was the last thing in the world that she expected to see. A few seconds later, she opened the door to the largest dog that she had ever seen. At some point in her educational career, she had written a report about different types of dog breeds, so she was almost certain that this was an English Sheepdog. Whatever it was, the animal was beautiful, and apparently well-trained, because it sat quietly on the porch, evidently waiting for her to do something.

Jamie loved dogs and she couldn't resist the temptation to kneel and pet the dog. The dog was very friendly, and after a few seconds of mutual nuzzling, she noticed that the dog was wearing a collar with a name tag attached to it. Just as she got a hold of the name tag, the sound of a high-pitched whistle floated through the air. The dog instantly became alert and turned around to look across the road. When the whistle sounded again, it took off at a run. After crossing the road, it shimmied under the wooden fence, bounded across the field, and disappeared into the woods. She watched for a moment to see if the animal would reappear, but it didn't.

After walking back into the house and sitting back down into the chair, she considered the possibility that she had dreamed the whole thing. However, when she got back up and looked at the porch, there were some muddy prints in front of the door that had not been there earlier.

The following Monday evening, just after dark, Jamie finished sewing some cushions for her new chair. After tying the pale blue cushions onto the rocker, she admired her work for a moment and then decided that she was satisfied. It was time for her favorite TV program, so she picked up the remote and sat down in the rocker. Just as the TV came to life, she heard a rumble of thunder, followed by a flash of light outside. That wasn't surprising, because the weather forecast had called for some thunderstorms, which could possibly be heavy.

A moment later, she heard the same thump at the door that she had heard the week before. This time she jumped up quickly and opened the door. Sure enough, there sat the same dog once again.

"Hey you," she said as she kneeled down and picked up his tag. This time she was able to read the words.

"Barney. Wilson Family Farms"

"Well, at least I know your name now," she told him as she began to pet him. There was another loud rumble of thunder at that point. Barney turned and looked across the road. Jamie thought that she heard the whistle again, but she couldn't be sure because the wind was blowing very hard, and it was making a roaring sound.

Suddenly, Barney once again turned and bounded across the road. It was very dark, so Jamie lost sight of him, but a few seconds later, lightning lit up the sky and during the flash, Jamie was totally stunned at what she saw. It appeared that right at the edge of the woods there was a either a young girl or boy wearing a cowboy hat sitting on a horse.

Did she really see that, or was the storm causing her imagination to run away with her? She waited for several minutes to see if the lightning would accommodate her by lighting up the woods again, but it didn't.

Chapter Two

Jamie did not see Barney again over the next couple of weeks. It took her a couple of days to shake off the vision of the horse rider that she may or may not have seen during the thunderstorm. Eventually, she convinced herself that the storm had played games with her imagination.

It was now the last week of July, so she decided that it was time to visit her new school.

She had met the principal, Tom Elliot, during her interview process. He had seemed like a nice man, and she hoped that he would be working in the building when she went in. Two of the other three second grade teachers had also participated in interviewing her. Both of them had seemed nice at the time, but she hadn't really been able to spend enough time with them to get a feel for what kind of teachers they were.

On this Monday morning, when she entered the office there were two women chatting at what appeared to be the secretary's desk. One of them looked familiar, but Jamie wasn't quite sure where she had seen her before.

"Good morning," the other woman who was seated at the desk spoke. "Is there something that I can help you with?"

Knowing that first impressions were important, Jamie tried to present her best smile. "Hello, I'm Jamie Barnes. I'm the new second grade teacher. Is Mr. Elliot in today?"

The woman at the desk stood and walked around to her. "Hi. I'm Sandy Fisher, the school secretary. Welcome. We are glad to have you.

Tom won't be in until tomorrow, but I'll be happy to show you around."

"Thank you," Jamie answered, relieved to receive a warm greeting.

Sandy turned and looked at the other woman. "This is Mary Wilson, our resident counselor and social worker."

Mary walked over to her and extended her hand. "It's nice to meet you," she said. "I understand that you are from Ohio."

"I'm from Grove City, which is not far from Columbus," she told her.

Hearing her reply, Mary's face lit up. I'm from Cambridge. Do I dare ask. Did you attend…"

Jamie grinned. "I did." She paused a moment and then said, "OH."

Mary immediately responded with, "IO"

At that same moment, Sandy let out a groan. "Oh no."

Then Mary leaned over closer to her and spoke with a quiet voice. "There are Wolverines among us." She was referring to the huge rivalry between the University of Michigan and Ohio State University.

"I'm so excited to have a buckeye friend," she said. "Sometimes during football season, I'm not allowed to eat in the teacher's lunchroom."

Sandy rolled her eyes. "Would you like to see your class list?"

"I would love to," Jamie answered.

A minute later, as she was looking at her list, Mary picked up her glasses off the desk and put them on. She asked Jamie if she could see the list and then she mentioned a couple of names of students that she had counseled in the past. While they were talking, it occurred to Jamie where she had seen Mary before. She was the woman seated in the diner with the man who had called her ma'am.

Then something else occurred to her. Her last name was Wilson. Could this be a connection to the Wilson Farms that Barney belonged to? Her curiosity got the better of her, so she decided to just ask.

"Are you related to the Wilsons of Wilson's farms?"

Mary laughed. "I guess that you could say that I am related to them. My husband and my son run the farm."

Jamie hesitated and then asked another question. "Would you possibly own a very large dog named Barney? Possibly an English Sheepdog?"

Mary studied her for a moment. "Did John and Carol rent you the house on Ranch Road?"

After she nodded, Mary continued. "Has Barney been visiting you? He used to go over there to see Carol's grandmother, Maggie. Even after she moved out, he continued to go over there when Ellen lived there. I think he was looking for Maggie."

"He has showed up a couple of times," Jamie told her. "I haven't seen him in a while though; not since that night about a week ago that we had that bad storm. Does someone call him with a whistle of some sort?"

"Yes," Mary answered. "He belongs to my daughter, Annie. He is trained to come when she blows the whistle."

Jamie thought for a moment. "Does your daughter ever ride a horse?"

"She does," Mary said. "Annie is quite an animal lover. Why do you ask?"

Jamie told her about what happened the night of the storm.

Mary's eyes narrowed. "I remember that night. My husband, Jake, and I were very upset with her because she shouldn't have been out on her horse in such bad weather. She and Barney came in looking like drowned rats. Her excuse was that she was worried about Barney. We told her that dogs can take care of themselves, but she had put herself and her horse in jeopardy. The grounding from her horse that she received just ended yesterday. I'll tell you what. I'll give you my phone number and if Barney comes to your house again, you can text me and I'll have Annie come to the woods and call him with the whistle."

"I would be happy to do that," Jamie said. "Is it far to your house?"

Mary smiled. "Our back yard is on the other side of the woods, so I guess that you could say that we are neighbors."

"How old is Annie?" Jamie asked her.

"Twelve going on twenty-five," Mary laughed. "When school starts, she will be in the sixth grade. I've always said that middle school is just something you have to live through. I guess that would also include the parents of the young adolescents." Before Jamie could respond to that statement, Sandy broke into their conversation.

"Mary, a Mrs. Ferris is returning your call."

"Oh good," she answered. "I'll take it in my office." Then she turned to Jamie. "We'll talk again soon."

After she left, Sandy smiled at Jamie. "I sent Tom a text and he said that I should show you around and give you the keys to your room. He also said that he has meetings all day at the board office, but he will definitely be in early tomorrow morning, and he is looking forward to seeing you again."

"Wonderful," Jamie answered.

For the next few minutes, Sandy gave her a tour of the building, which ended at her room, which was in a nice location. It was halfway down the hall from the office and close to the bathrooms. The rooms were set up in pods of two. The door next to hers looked bare and dark.

"Your pod partner is Leslie Mitchell," Sandy told her. "Did you meet her during the interview process?"

"No, I did not," Jamie replied. "I met Kim and Gina, but I believe Leslie was possibly out of town."

Sandy nodded. "Leslie had to go to Green Bay to see a family member who had taken a bad fall or something. Anyway, you will love Leslie. She has one of those larger-than-life personalities, and I'm sure that she will help you in any way that she can."

"I'm glad to hear that," Jamie told her. "I'm sure that I will have lots of questions." She let out a small laugh. "I hope that I don't make a nuisance of myself."

Sandy smiled as she unlocked the door. "I am sure that there is no way that you will annoy Leslie. As a matter of fact, I fully expect her to show up today." She then opened the door and flipped on the lights.

As the room lit up, a sense of warmth and excitement flowed through Jamie. The room was bare but clean. The student desks were all pushed to one side of the room with the chairs piled on them, while the teacher desk had been pushed against another wall with an adult sized desk chair sitting on top of it. There was a horseshoe table turned upside down next to the student desks, with small chairs stacked on top of it.

Obviously, there was a lot of work to be done, but at long last she was the captain of her own ship, and all the decisions were hers and hers alone. That was what was causing the sudden happiness that swelled through her.

Sandy seemed to understand this moment, because she handed Jamie her keys and said, "It's all yours. Enjoy." Then she turned to leave, but she stopped and added one more thing. "If you need anything, just ask. My extension is 152."

"Thank you," Jamie answered, as she ventured further into the room.

The next thing she did was to pull her chair off the desk and sit down on it. It was a comfortable swivel chair which was adjustable. After a moment, she decided that her desk should be located near the phone. There was also an empty table that she assumed would be a good place for the laptop computer that Sandy had explained that the IT person would assign to her later in the week.

The desk was metal, but as Jamie tried to move it, she realized that it wasn't heavy, but it was awkward. While she was contemplating how to move it across the floor, which appeared to be rather new, she heard a voice coming from the doorway.

"I have been begging the maintenance people for years to put things back to where they were to begin with, but every year they leave us a mess to deal with."

Jamie looked up at the woman who was standing in the doorway. Later, it would occur to her that the best way to describe Leslie was that she was a 5-foot 4-inch package of energy. Her ginger hair was cut in a short bob style and her brown eyes were as warm as her smile. She was dressed in worn but comfortable-looking denim shorts and a faded green T-shirt along with a pair of tennis shoes that appeared to be well broken in. There was a large teacher bag strapped across her shoulder.

"Hello," Jamie said. "You must be Leslie."

"I am," she answered, moving on into the classroom. "And you are Jamie. Sandy told me that you were here. It's nice to finally meet you."

"It's nice to meet you too," Jamie answered as she shook her hand.

"Let me open my door and put my bag down, and then I'll help you with your desk," she said.

An hour later, Jamie understood what Sandy had meant about Leslie, and she knew that she had found a friend. By lunchtime the two of them had managed to move both of their desks across their rooms and had also arranged Leslie's student desks. They moved hers first because Jamie wasn't sure exactly what kind of formation that she wanted to use. Once Leslie's room was arranged, it was easier to see what some of the possibilities were.

The two of them decided to stop at that point and have some lunch. They went to the same little diner that Jamie had had lunch at the day that she had bought the chair. As they ate, Leslie gave her the low down on everyone at the school. The interesting thing was that she didn't have a lot to say about Kim and Gina. She didn't seem to have a dislike of them, but she just said that they were both excellent teachers. However, they each had small children at home, so they had to be very organized so that they didn't have to spend too much extra time at school.

She had very favorable things to say about Sandy and Mary. That reminded Jamie of her encounter with Mary and the man who Jamie thought was her son. When she told Leslie about how she was bothered by the fact that she was called "ma'am", Leslie laughed.

"You have never been called that before?" she asked.

"No," she said. "and it made me feel old."

"Oh honey, that's just the country manners that he was taught by Jake and Mary. Don't worry about that. I think Chris is an ass, anyway."

"Because he called me ma'am?"

"No, he just is."

"Do you know him?" Jamie asked out of curiosity.

"We went to high school together," Leslie told her. "He wasn't so bad then. He was very popular, and a little spoiled, but kind of a nice guy."

"But now he is a jerk?" Jamie asked. "What happened?"

Leslie rolled her eyes. "The classic story. Boy meets beautiful girl. Girl wraps him around her little finger. Boy catches her cheating, kicks her to the curb, and then buries himself in his work and becomes bitter to the world."

That story had an all too familiar ring to it, and Jamie had a sudden wave of compassion for Chris Wilson. "It sounds like he's better off without her."

"He is," Leslie replied, "but it still stings."

"It sure does," Jamie agreed and then changed the subject. "There certainly is quite an age difference between Chris and Annie."

"Yes," Leslie answered and then she paused before continuing. "I think that the best way to describe it is that Annie's arrival was a surprise to all of them."

"I guess," Jamie said and looked at her phone. "We've been here nearly an hour. I'd like to get back to school and put in a couple of more hours today."

The afternoon flew by as did the rest of the week. By Friday afternoon, her room was arranged, the name tags were on the desks and her bulletin boards were covered. Her plan for the next week was to spend at least an hour every day studying the 2nd grade outcomes for the state of Wisconsin and write her lesson plans for the first couple of weeks of school.

When she got home on Friday evening, she was very tired. While at lunch with Leslie and Sandy that day, she had had the foresight to order a large Hoagie, so that she had leftovers for dinner. After she finished eating it, she turned on the TV and stretched out on the couch.

When she heard the now familiar thud at the door, she sat up quickly, realizing that she had fallen asleep, and that Barney's arrival had woken her up. She went to look out the window and confirmed that it was him. This time when she opened the door, he bounded right in and sat in front of the rocker.

"All righty then," Jamie said and then she picked up her phone. She sent Mary a simple text message. *"Barney's here."*

A couple of minutes later, Mary replied. *"My son, Chris, is on his way home. He is going to stop and get him in about 5 minutes."*

"This will be interesting," Jamie said to herself.

When Jamie saw the truck lights turn into her driveway, she opened the door and said, "Come on Barney. Chris is here to take you home."

The dog just stared at her and didn't move a muscle. Chris got out of his truck and walked onto the porch. Jamie smiled at him and said, "Hello."

He nodded without saying anything directly to her. At least this time, he didn't call her ma'am.

"Umm, he doesn't seem to want to move," Jamie told him. "He came in when I opened the door, and then when I opened it again, and called him, he just looked at me."

Chris stared in the door at the dog. "Let's go Barney," he said in an authoritative voice. Barney stared back at him as if he were deciding how far he could push the situation.

Deciding to try a new tactic, Chris spoke again. "I think Mom bought some ice cream today." That did it. Barney sprinted out the door and didn't stop until he got to the truck and leaped inside through the open door and sat on the passenger seat waiting to be driven home for his ice cream.

Jamie couldn't help but laugh at that point. Chris, however, was not amused. "I'm sorry about this," he said. "I hope he wasn't too much of a nuisance."

"Not at all," she answered. "I love dogs, and Barney is an absolutely beautiful one."

"He is an absolutely spoiled one," Chris replied as he turned to go back to his truck. "Thank you. Have a good one."

Once he was gone, Jamie shut the door and contemplated Leslie 's description of Chris Wilsom. From what little she saw of him tonight, she wouldn't exactly describe him as an ass, but she also wouldn't say that he was overly friendly.

After a large yawn, she decided that maybe it was time to turn in. She then picked up the remote and switched off the television. Just as she was about to turn off the lamp, she noticed something that made her stop and stare.

The cushions that she had made for the rocking chair had ties that were used to fasten them to the chair both at the top and the bottom. What she noticed was that the tie in the upper left-hand corner had come untied. Jamie was positive that she had tied them very tightly. That was strange. After a moment of staring, she finally shrugged and retied them, this time very securely.

The next morning, Jamie drove to a mall that Carol had told her about that was just outside of Madison. Much to her disappointment, Carol had several music lessons scheduled that afternoon and she was unable to go with her. Leslie, it turned out. had a boyfriend who lived in Milwaukee, and she spent most of her weekends there. After some thought, Jamie decided that maybe it was better that she went alone, because she would be able to focus more on her shopping for new school clothes.

By lunchtime, Jamie was the owner of three new tops, two skirts, and a couple of summer dresses that were on sale. She still needed to look for some new shoes, but her stomach was beginning to growl, so she decided to take a break at the food court. While she was deciding which restaurant to purchase her lunch from, she happened to notice Mary and a young girl, who must have been Annie, standing in line at the Chinese restaurant.

She smiled and approached her friend. "I was wondering what the best place for lunch was. Since you are in line here, I guess this must be a good choice.

Mary turned around and smiled. "Well, hello Jamie." Then she introduced her to her daughter. "This is Barney's new friend," Mary explained to Annie."

The girl giggled. "Sorry about that, but I'm sure he will be back."

"It's not a problem," Jamie answered. "I love dogs and Barney seems to be a sweetheart."

"He is," Annie agreed.

"Well, tell me what's good here," Jamie asked the two of them.

"Everything," Annie quickly responded. "You can't go wrong with anything on this menu."

"Good to know," she replied.

Fifteen minutes later, the three of them were seated at a table enjoying an assortment of different oriental dishes that they had ordered with the plan of sharing.

"Did you find any good sales?" Mary asked. Jamie told her about the purchases that she had made.

"Are you all set for school then?" Mary wanted to know.

"I still need to look for some shoes," she answered. "Then I'm going to get some supplies for my Cricut, because I think that I want to make some decorations for my bulletin boards."

As soon as the words were out of her mouth, Annie's face lit up. "You have a Cricut?" she asked. "I've been wanting one for about a year now, but Mom isn't sure whether I would use it enough to make it worthwhile."

Jamie smiled. "I do, and I love it."

"What kind of things do you make with it?" Annie asked.

"Well, let's see. I've made quite a few t-shirts, and some ornaments," she said. "When I was a substitute teacher, I became somewhat of a go to person for making decorations and labels. I never minded though as long as they bought the supplies."

"Do you think that you could help me make some t-shirts for my friends and me?" Annie stole a look at her mother who was quietly watching the exchange between the two of them. "We could get the t-shirts and supplies, couldn't we Mom?"

Mary smiled. "We could do that, but I'm sure that Jamie is very busy getting ready for the start of the school year. Maybe it would be better to wait until after school is well underway."

The girl's face immediately fell, and Jamie suddenly felt a little sympathy or maybe empathy for her. "I am doing well staying on task," she said, "and maybe I need a little diversion from school projects. Would you like to come with me to the craft store and we can talk about some ideas for your shirts?"

Annie's face lit up once more. "Could I Mom? Please?"

Mary looked over at Jamie. "Are you sure about this?"

"It's fine," she answered. "It'll be fun. I love crafting."

Two hours later, Mary met Jamie and her daughter back at the food court. Annie was beside herself with excitement about the plan that she and Jamie had come up with to make t-shirts for her and her friends to wear on the first day of school. She couldn't wait to get hold of her mother's phone to call her friends to find out their t-shirt sizes so that they could stop at the Dollar General on the way home to buy shirts.

While she was taking care of that, Mary and Jamie had a discussion about when the best time to work on this project would be. Jamie offered to have Annie come over the next afternoon, which was a Sunday. Her theory was that it would be just as well to finish it sooner rather than later, because otherwise they would never hear the end of it until it was done.

That night Jamie spent several hours working on decorations and labels for her classroom. It was very late when she finished, and as she came out of her spare room, she realized that she was hungry, so she decided to fix a late-night snack before going to bed. On her way to the kitchen, she passed through the living room. Just as she reached the doorway, she stopped, because it occurred to her that something wasn't right. After a few seconds, she turned around and stared at the living room. Taking a few steps back into the room, she stood and stared. It took a moment for her to realize what was different, and at that point a small chill went through her.

After another moment of staring, she pulled the rocking chair back about three feet to the position that she had originally placed it in. The logical part of her mind tried to tell her that she had probably accidentally pushed it at some point without realizing it. Then she shook off the entire incident and went to bed, completely forgetting about the idea of fixing a snack.

The next afternoon, Mary brought a very excited Annie to her house. Barney also came along, and Mary apologized, but Annie insisted that he come, saying he would just show up anyway. Jamie had to agree that the girl was probably right.

After Mary left, the two of them immediately got started on the project. They worked for about an hour, and then they took a break before preparing to begin ironing the design on the shirts. The two of them headed into the kitchen to have a quick snack. Jamie laughed because Barney was still sitting in the same spot that he had been in since he arrived, right in front of the rocking chair.

Annie giggled. "Barney always sits there because that was Maggie's favorite place to sit. He liked to sit in front of her. I think that he misses her."

"Carol's grandmother?" Jamie asked.

The girl nodded. "Yes, she loved sitting in that chair."

Jamie smiled and then after a second, she frowned. "Do you mean that Maggie had a rocking chair in that same spot?"

Now Annie gave her a confused look. "No, I'm talking about *that* rocking chair," she said. "I think that it is pretty old. I'm not sure, but I think maybe I heard somebody say it was Maggie's mother's or something."

"No," Jamie began to explain. "When I moved in here, the only furniture in the room was the couch and an old worn-out recliner. It wouldn't even recline, so Carol's sons took it to the dump. I bought that rocking chair in an antique store in town. It had been painted white, so I paid a man at the hardware store to refinish it."

Annie just stared at her for a moment before speaking. "Then you must have found the cushions in a closet or something."

Now Jamie just shook her head. "No, I made them with material that I bought at the Walmart in Valene."

The look that Annie then gave her was hard to describe. "I know that I wasn't very old when Maggie moved out of here, but the cushions that were on that chair were almost exactly like the ones that you made."

"Hmm," Jamie said. "That is a weird coincidence." Then for some unknown reason, she decided to change the subject. "Let's get some iced tea."

Later that night, as Jamie was lying on her couch staring at the rocking chair, she decided to call Carol. They chatted for a while and then Jamie casually brought up the subject of the rocking chair. She told her the story of how she had come to acquire it and then she finished with what Annie had told her that afternoon.

Carol was quiet for a moment before she responded. "Grandma did have a rocking chair in the living room that she absolutely loved. She wanted to take it with her to the assisted living, but unfortunately there wasn't any room there because we had to get her an electronic lift chair, because she can no longer get up and down out of chairs by herself. I was going to take the rocking chair to my home, but my mother...who was not exactly a sentimental person, had a yard sale to get rid of most of the things in the home. Unfortunately, the chair was sold in the sale. Mother claimed that it was just a mistake, but I'm not so sure. Anyway, she and I had quite a row over it."

"Oh my, that's very sad," Jamie said.

"Yes, it is," Carol replied. "Now I am curious though. Is it possible that whoever bought the chair ended up painting it and then not liking it, so they sold it to the antique store?"

Jamie thought for a moment and then suddenly remembered something which she told Carol. "There was a place on the back of one of the legs where someone had tried to scrape the paint off the chair. That's how Earl knew what the original stain looked like."

"Hmm," Carol answered. "That is interesting. I need to look through some photo albums because I believe there is a picture of the chair somewhere. Let me look around and see if I can find one."

"And in the meantime, I will take one of this one and send it to you," Jamie told her. "Maybe we can figure out if the chair found its way home."

As soon as they finished talking, Jamie took several pictures of the chair from different angles. Then after a moment of thought, she took the cushions off and took some more. After sending all the pictures to Carol, she carefully replaced the cushions.

Two hours later, just as she was climbing into bed, her phone pinged. Picking it up, she saw that it was a text message from Carol. The message contained no words, just one picture of the chair. For a moment she was confused, because she thought that Carol had sent one of her pictures back. Then she realized that in this picture the wall behind the chair was not painted, but it was covered with flowered wallpaper. If not for that, it could have been the same picture. The chair looked exactly the same, and the cushions appeared to be made of the same material.

Chapter Three

    The following week was the last one before the beginning of the school year, and the school building was a beehive of activity. Jamie was finally able to reconnect with Kim and Gina. The two of them came in early each morning and worked diligently and then left by lunchtime. Jamie had a few brief conversations with them, but she hated to disturb them too much because she knew that their time was limited.

    Gina seemed to be a little more outgoing than Kim, but both of them offered to help Jamie in any way that they could. On Friday morning of that week, the four of them had an extended grade level meeting in which they discussed some shared units and their duty schedules. By the end of the meeting, Jamie had a good feeling about the coming school year.

After the meeting, Gina and Kim went home and Jamie went to lunch with Leslie at the diner in town. While they were eating, Jamie told her friend the strange story about the chair. Leslie sat staring at her until she was finished talking. Then she made an interesting comment.

"I have an idea who may have bought the chair at the yard sale."

"Really?" Jamie asked. "Who?"

"It's not anyone that you know," Leslie said. "Let me do some checking and I'll get back to you on it."

Before Jamie could respond, she noticed the door of the diner opening and then Chris Wilson walked in. As he passed by their table, he stopped and spoke politely to them. Then he looked directly at Jamie and spoke.

"You haven't been visited by our goofy dog lately, have you?" he asked.

Jamie laughed. "I love your goofy dog," she told him, "and the only time that he has been around has been when he has come with Annie. We have been working on some craft projects, and he just sits in the living room in front of the rocking chair."

Chris rolled his eyes. "My sister is another one. The girl can be a little chatterbox. If she makes too much of a nuisance of herself, just send her home. She probably won't stay, but it might be the only way you can get some peace."

"Annie is fine," Jamie told him. "Truthfully, she has been helping me with some of my school projects, so I can't complain about that."

"Well, I'm glad that she is earning her keep," he said. Then he turned to Leslie. "How is your brother doing?"

"Mark's doing well," she answered. "He is still in Colorado, and he and his wife just had their 4th child. They now have two boys and two girls."

"Good Lord," he said. "That is a lot of family. The next time you talk to him, you tell him I said hi and good luck."

"I will," Leslie replied. "Joe and I are talking about going out there over Thanksgiving."

Then Chris nodded at them and said, "You ladies have a nice afternoon."

After a moment, Leslie spoke. "That was interesting."

"Why?" Jamie wanted to know.

"He was almost human."

The following Tuesday was the first day of school. Jamie was so nervous that she barely slept the night before. Although she ran on adrenaline most of the day, everything worked out well. The day ran smoothly with only minimal problems. At the end of the day, once the buses of students had departed, the four second grade teachers stood in the hallway outside their rooms and reviewed the day. Jamie felt a sense of satisfaction and excitement about the school year that loomed in front of them.

An hour later, once she felt that everything was in order for the next day, she took her teacher bag and headed toward the parking lot. Just as she unlocked her car door, she heard someone calling her name. She looked up to see Mary coming toward her, so she stopped to wait for her.

"I've been crazy busy today," she said, "but I wanted to know how your day went."

Jamie smiled. "I had a fantastic day," she answered. "Everything went well."

"I'm glad to hear that," Mary said. "My theory is that how well the first day goes is an indication of how the entire year will go."

"Good to know," Jamie replied.

"I wanted to ask you about something else," Mary continued. "Annie's birthday is Saturday, and we are going to grill some hamburgers and have ice cream and cake. She is inviting a few of her friends over and she wanted me to ask you to come so her friends could meet the lady who helped her with the t-shirts."

"Oh, that is very sweet of her to think of me," Jamie said. "Would you like me to bring something?"

"No, I think that I have it covered," Mary told her. "We are going to grill around six, but you can come anytime."

A warmth spread through Jamie at being included. "Thank you. I will look forward to that."

"Wonderful," Mary said. "I don't mean to be rude, but Jake needs my help with something at home, and I'm anxious to see how Annie's first day of middle school went. I'm sure that I will see you tomorrow." She then got into her car and drove off with a wave.

The rest of the week flew by and before Jamie knew it, it was Friday afternoon and her first week of teaching was behind her. As she stood in the hallway at the end of the day with her teaching partners, she realized one problem. Forgetting to go to the shoe store at the mall had been a mistake. She definitely needed some new shoes, because her feet were aching. Another trip to the mall in the morning was certainly in order.

While she was there, she could also pick up a birthday present for Annie.

Right after Kim and Gina went into their rooms to collect their things to go home, she turned to Leslie and then reached down and took her shoes off with a grimace. Her friend laughed and then gave her some advice about how to soak her feet that night and what kind of shoes offered the best support.

The next morning at the mall, she was easily able to find the shoes that Leslie had recommended and as she slid her feet into them, she sighed because her feet felt as good as they had in the last week. She purchased three pairs and then headed to the craft store where she bought various supplies that could be used in a Cricut, in case Mary decided to give her one for her birthday. If not, she could offer to let her use the supplies on her machine.

She arrived at the Wilson home around five. She was surprised to see that she only had to drive a few yards from her driveway, make one right turn and then it was a very short distance to the Wilson house. Jamie had expected it to be a ranch type home, but it was actually a two-story brick home with a large front porch. There was a garage attached to the house, and then there was another unattached garage on the other side of the driveway. It was also a two-story building with two large-looking bays on the bottom.

Jamie parked her car and then looked at the house and wondered if she should go to the front or back door. It appeared as if the party was set up on the covered back porch, so she moved in that direction. Just as she stepped onto the walkway, Mary came out of the back door onto the porch.

"Hi," she said. "You're early, thank goodness. I could use some help setting up. Jake went to pick up his mother in Valene and he took Annie with him. Apparently, he had a flat tire on the way, and they are going to be cutting it close. Chris had to go to Madison to pick up some kind of medicine or something for one of the horses, so as usual I'm left holding the bag."

"I'd be glad to help," Jamie said with a smile. "Just tell me what to do. I guess it's one of those days where everything is happening at once."

Mary sighed. "That seems to be every day in my life."

Forty-five minutes later, Jake and Annie returned with his mother. Jake was a tall burly man who looked like an older version of Chris. His mother was a small frail looking woman who they led immediately to a chair on the porch which was apparently her special chair.

When she was introduced to Nora Wilson, Jamie smiled and shook her hand. The smile that the woman returned gave her a strange feeling almost as if the woman knew something about her. After a few seconds, Jamie shook the feeling off, attributing it to the fact that the woman was old.

A moment later, the first of Annie's friends arrived and Jake lit the grill. The party was getting underway. Apparently, it was going to be a slumber party because each girl arrived with a well stuffed backpack and a sleeping bag. There was lots of giggling and discussion about what they were planning for the early morning hours. Jamie saw Jake and Mary exchange a look that most likely meant, *"It's going to be a long night"*. She smiled to herself and wondered if girls still did some of the same things that she did at slumber parties when she was young. If they did, Mary had better sleep with one ear open.

Just as the hamburgers were done, Chris called and said that he had gone to two places for the medicine that he was looking for and was now headed to a third, hoping to get there before it closed. Jamie thought that Mary didn't seem pleased about that, but there was nothing that she could do.

Once dinner was over, it was time to open the presents. Annie opened all her friends' gifts first. There was a variety of early teenage girl gifts, such as jewelry, make-up, and a couple of sets of silly socks. When she opened Jamie's gift, all the girls were excited, and immediately began to giggle about the things that she could make that would benefit all of them. Earlier while she was helping Mary set up for the party, Jamie had questioned Mary about whether they were going to get Annie a Cricut for her birthday. She had explained that she and Jake had given her a choice of receiving the Cricut or upgrading her phone to an iPhone. Evidently, after much somewhat dramatic agonizing, she had decided on the phone, because she knew that she could use Jamie's machine this fall and then hope for a Cricut for Christmas.

She opened the phone last and then there was more squealing and several minutes of installing numbers and some texting back and forth among her friends. Just as that excitement died down Chris finally arrived. As he walked onto the back porch, Jamie noticed a couple of things. One was that all of Annie's friends looked up at him in a sort of adolescent worship. She imagined that several of the girls did have a little bit of a crush on their friend's older brother. The other thing that was apparent was that Chris looked very tired.

"I'm sorry that I'm late kiddo," he said, "but it couldn't be helped." Then he reached into his shirt pocket and pulled out a card, which he handed to her. "Happy Birthday, Sis."

Annie tore open the envelope and politely read the card, before pulling a gift card out of a smaller envelope. It was in the amount of fifty dollars and could be used anywhere in the mall that Jamie had bought the Cricut supplies. Now there was more squealing and giggling along with discussion on which store that she could use it in.

When the chattering began, Chris immediately distanced himself from it, by first walking over to give his grandmother a kiss on the cheek and then walking over to the food table hoping to find something to eat. Mary got up and went to him and pointed to the kitchen, apparently telling him where she had put the food that she had saved for him, because he went inside and returned a couple of minutes later with a plate of food. He sat down in the corner, out of the way and quietly ate his food. When he finished, he got up and announced that he was going to the barn to take care of the ailing horse.

After a while, the girls took all of Annie's new treasures and their belongings upstairs to her room. The porch was now blessedly calm, and the four remaining adults talked quietly for a few minutes. When Jake saw his mother begin to yawn, he asked her if she was ready to go home. She smiled and said that she was beginning to tire, so he said he would pull the car out of the garage. After he left, Mary went into the house and got some leftovers she had saved to send home with her. Jake returned and helped his mother up and began walking her toward the car. As they passed Jamie, she stood and told the woman how nice it had been to meet her.

Nora smiled and said, "It was nice to meet you too, dear." Then she began walking with her son again, but then suddenly, she stopped, turned, and spoke again. "Be sure to take care of that chair." Then she turned back and continued her walk. Jamie stood there a moment, confused by the woman's words. After a moment, she turned to Mary, who was smiling.

"Nora is getting older, and she gets confused sometimes," she said. "I wouldn't pay much attention to her."

Jamie nodded, but something about the woman's words bothered her for reasons that she didn't quite understand. Then Mary said something else that surprised her.

"In her younger years, Nora was known in Valene as a sort of psychic or medium. She had an ability to foresee the future and supposedly give people messages from the other side."

At her words, a chill went through Jamie that she didn't quite understand. What bothered her was the mention of the chair. Was Nora talking about the rocking chair?

At that moment Chris came walking back from the barn and called out to his father. "Dad, do you want me to drive her home?"

Jake turned around and spoke to his son. "No, that's all right. I'll take her. Why don't you stay here and help your mother clean up? It looks like there is a storm coming. You all better get a move on." Jamie looked up at the darkening sky and saw what he was talking about.

"Will do," Chris answered. The three of them then began to quickly gather up things and carry them inside.

They got the last of the party items in the house just as the first loud crack of thunder was heard. Barney came bounding in with the loud noise and set himself on the floor in front of the refrigerator.

Mary sighed. "All right, you crazy dog. You can have some ice cream." She picked up the container off the table and scooped some into his bowl before putting the carton in the freezer. At that moment the sound of Annie calling for her mother could be heard from upstairs. Mary let out another sigh and began walking towards the stairs.

Jamie looked over at Chris, who was dropping dirty silverware into the sink while the water was running to fill it. "Can I help?" she asked, as she walked on into the kitchen.

Chris looked at her for a few seconds and then tossed her a dish towel. "I'll wash, you dry," he told her.

The two of them worked quietly for a few minutes, before Jamie broke the silence. "Your grandmother seems like a nice lady," she said. "Does she live alone?"

"Granny lives in a senior apartment complex where they have people come in and check on them every day," he told her. "She is in her nineties, has some arthritis and she doesn't see well, but her mind is as sharp as a tack."

Jamie frowned at his words. "I thought your mom said that she gets confused at times."

Chris looked over at her and grinned. "Why? What did Granny say?"

She told him about what Nora said to her as she walked out. Chris didn't reply immediately, but after a minute, he said, "Granny can be a little different at times, but I have learned that sometimes when she says strange things that don't make sense at the time, sooner or later, you will understand what her words meant. Mom doesn't want to buy into it, so she plays it off by saying that Granny is confused."

"But you do buy into it?" Jamie asked.

Again, he hesitated. "I know that several years ago, she warned me that I was making a mistake by trusting someone close to me. Mom told me not to pay any attention to her, so I didn't."

"And your grandmother was right?"

"She sure as hell was," he answered.

At that moment, Mary returned to the kitchen, and she was laughing about the fact that they had requested to light a candle so that they could hold a séance. She had dug around in a closet until she found a battery operated one.

"I guess that Granny left too soon," Chris said with a grin.

Mary just looked at him and shook her head. Then she swatted him with a dish towel that she had just picked up.

Later that night when Jamie returned home, she walked into the living room and stood and stared at the rocking chair. A moment later, she sat down in it and began to rock. After a couple of minutes of rocking, a sense of peacefulness flooded over her, and she began to drift off to sleep.

The sun was shining brightly as she walked down the road. As she was approaching a large new-looking house, she noticed that the front door was opening, and a very small little girl came running out the door.

"Mommy!" the child called out and began to run toward her. Just as the girl reached her with her arms held up, Jamie woke up and realized that she had fallen asleep in the rocking chair.

"*What a strange dream,*" she thought. After a moment, she decided that it was definitely time to go to bed. Fifteen minutes later, she was in bed and falling asleep once more. The rest of Jamie's night was peaceful and dreamless.

The next couple of weeks were very busy for Jamie as she began to grow into a routine with her young students. Things were going well in the second grade, but she knew that Mary's start to the year was not going so well. From what Jamie gathered some students had told her about some things in their counseling sessions that Mary had had to report to children's services, and ultimately the children had been removed from their homes. It was an unfortunate situation for everyone involved, but Jamie had had enough experience in being around these situations at schools, to know that Mary would be very upset.

Evidently, Jake must have understood that also, because he and Mary decided to take a last-minute weekend trip to Lake Mendota. As soon as Annie learned that she would be stuck with her brother the entire weekend, she called Jamie and asked if she could come over Saturday afternoon and do some crafting. Jamie told her that she was more than welcome.

Annie and Barney walked through the woods and arrived just before it began to rain very heavily. "Oh my," Jamie said. "It's supposed to rain all evening. I can run you home in my car later."

"Chris will come and get me," Annie answered.

"I know you want to make some crafts," Jamie told her, "but do you know what else I like to do on rainy days?"

"What?"

"I like to bake," she answered. "Would you like to make some cookies?"

"I would love to," Annie said.

An hour later, the last batch of chocolate chip cookies were in the oven, and they began to think about what would be good to have for dinner. After searching through the refrigerator, and looking through Pinterest, they decided to make homemade sloppy joes and French fries. As Jamie was cutting potatoes and watching Annie brown the ground beef, she asked her what her brother was doing that afternoon.

"He's running errands for Granny," she said. "Mom or Dad usually do that on Saturdays, but Chris gets the job today."

"Ah, so by coming here, you got out of all the running around?" Jamie asked with a smile.

Annie giggled. "Well, Mom usually orders her groceries online, so she just had to be dropped off at her hair salon, then he had to get some things at the drug store, pick up her groceries and go put them away. After that he will go pick her up and then take her wherever she wants to go for dinner."

"Aww. That makes a nice afternoon for her, doesn't it?" Jamie asked.

"Yeah, I have to go sometimes when Mom takes her," Annie told her. "The dinner part is kind of boring because Mom and her talk about old time stuff. I'm always anxious for it to be over. Then I feel bad because I know that someday she will be gone, and I will be sorry I didn't have a better attitude."

"I understand," Jamie told her. "I had a grandmother when I was your age, and she was old and not well. I dreaded going to see her."

"Did she die?" Annie asked.

"Yes," Jamie answered. "She died in her sleep in a nursing home when I was sixteen. I wasn't really all that sad, and then I felt guilty about that, but my mother told me not to, because she was in a better place."

Annie's phone beeped, so she turned the meat down and picked up her phone. After a minute, she set the phone down and said, "Chris just picked Granny up from the salon and they are going to Burton's Café." Then she giggled.

"What's so funny?" Jamie wanted to know.

"Burton's Café is this little place that Granny loves, but it's pretty awful. The food is greasy and is usually either raw or burned. Chris hates it. Can I tell him not to eat much because we are making food here?"

"Sure," Jamie answered. "We will have plenty."

After they finished their dinner, the two of them went to the craft room and went through the bag of supplies that Jamie had given Annie for her birthday. They discussed the possibility of making some jewelry, but they decided that it was too late to begin that night. Jamie told her young friend they could work on it the next weekend if she would like.

"You don't have a boyfriend, do you?" Annie suddenly asked.

Somewhat surprised by the question, Jamie knew that her face turned red as she said, "No. I don't."

"I bet you have had one though, haven't you?" Annie wanted to know.

Not wanting to go into the details of her past romances with a thirteen-year-old, Jamie gave her a brief answer and then changed the subject. "I've had a few in my day. I imagine that Chris will be here before long."

Annie studied her for a moment, and Jamie was almost certain that she was going to pursue the subject of her past love life, but the sound of a door shutting outside prevented that. They both stood and walked back to the living room just as Chris reached the front door. Annie let him in and the three of them went to the kitchen.

Jamie reheated some food for him, and while he ate, his sister questioned him about his afternoon.

"What did you order at Burton's?" she asked with a grin.

Chris sighed. "I ordered a bowl of vegetable soup."

"How was it?"

The look he gave her was the answer to her question. "When Granny went to the bathroom, the waitress came by, and I gave her my half-eaten bowl telling her that I wasn't hungry. That way Granny couldn't insist that I take my leftovers home."

"Waste not, want not," Annie said with a giggle. Chris smiled back at her. Apparently, this was an old joke.

"This is a really good sloppy joe," Chris said, looking at Jamie.

"We found the recipe on Pinterest," Annie told him. "I made the sandwich mixture and Jamie made the fries. We made chocolate chip cookies too."

"Awesome," he replied. "I'm starving. I told Granny that I had a big lunch, but the truth was that all I had was some beef jerky that I grabbed at the drug store. All of this is really good. Jamie, it was nice of you to entertain Annie all afternoon and to feed both of us."

She smiled. "I enjoy the time that Annie and I spend together. We didn't do much crafting today, but the cooking was fun, wasn't it?"

"Yes, it was," the girl answered with a smile.

Chris finished the food on his plate and then reached over to the cookie dish and selected two of the gooey treats.

"Are we going to go to brunch tomorrow?" Annie asked him.

"It's either that or you are cooking," he answered, before taking another bite of cookie.

She then turned to Jamie and spoke. "Do you want to go with us? We go to the Sunday Brunch at this country club outside of Valene. It is massive and the food is to die for."

At that point, Jamie felt a little awkward. The invitation sounded nice, but she wasn't sure how Chris would feel about her tagging along with them. She was trying to think of a graceful out when Chris solved the issue.

"Sure, why don't you come with us?" he said. "Annie's right. The food is great. We can all go and eat a whole day's worth of food. Then we will charge it to Dad's account. It's kind of a family tradition that we go there most Sundays anyway. Sometimes we take Granny, but she told me that she didn't want to go tomorrow, so it would just be the three of us. What do you say?"

Before she could respond, Annie's cell phone suddenly sprang to life. It was Mary checking in. Annie updated her mother on her afternoon and evening right up to the point where they had just invited Jamie to brunch. Annie listened for a moment and then said goodbye to her mother.

"Mom said that absolutely we should all go to brunch tomorrow and to charge it to their account," she reported.

Chris and Annie both looked at Jamie, so she smiled and said, "Well I guess that settles it. We are going to brunch tomorrow."

The next morning, Chris and Annie picked Jamie up around 10:00. It took about twenty minutes to get to the country club. When they entered the dining area, Jamie was amazed. She had never seen such a large buffet in her life.

They were seated near a large window that had a nice view of the golf course. After they were served their coffee, the three of them walked over to the buffet area. Jamie looked around, not sure where to begin.

Annie laughed and said, "Follow me."

A few minutes later, the three of them were seated again and they began to enjoy the delicious food. It was quiet for a few minutes and then Jamie brought up a subject that she had been wondering about since Annie's birthday party.

"There is something that I wanted to ask you all about," she began. "Chris, you and I talked briefly about this after Annie's party, but I am a little curious about your grandmother's ...ability to see or I guess know things."

"How did you hear about that?" Annie asked.

"Your mother mentioned it to me," Jamie answered. Then she told her about how Nora had told her to take care of the chair.

At her words, Annie stopped eating for a moment and just stared at her. Chris, however, asked her a question.

"Explain this chair business to me," he said.

Jamie told him the whole story from when she bought the rocker at the antique store and how Earl had restored it. She then told him about how she had made cushions for it and that Annie had thought that it was the original chair. Then she showed them both the picture that Carol had sent her along with the photo that she had taken of her chair.

Chris was the first to speak after studying the pictures. "So, I guess the question is whether or not it is the same chair."

"It would seem to be," she answered. "It could be just a strange coincidence, but what really spooked me was your grandmother telling me to take care of the chair. It actually kind of sent a chill through me."

"That is strange," Chris said. "Some of the things that she comes up with are really out there, but once in a while, she hits the nail on the head."

Annie looked at her brother. "Like when she warned you about Cassie?"

Chris stared at her for a moment and then said, "I'm going to get some more food."

When he was safely gone, Annie explained. "Chris had this girlfriend that he was totally in love with and one day she just dumped him for somebody else. He was totally devastated. Granny had tried to warn him, but I guess he didn't listen. He was a mess for a long time after that. As far as I know, he hasn't taken any girls out since. I wish he would find some nice girl, but I guess it must be hard to get over something like that."

Jamie responded out loud before she realized what she was saying. "It certainly is."

Annie was giving her a strange look and then Chris returned. The waitress came right after that and refilled their coffees. When she was gone, Chris made a surprising statement.

"I guess if we want to know what Granny meant, there is only one thing to do," he said.

"What's that?" Jamie asked.

"We'll just have to ask her."

Chapter Four

"Let's go right now!" Annie exclaimed with the typical passion of a young adolescent.

Chris looked at his watch. "I don't know," he answered. "I've got some work to do in the barn this afternoon.

"I'm afraid I can't either," Jamie added. "I have a Zoom call with some friends from Ohio at 3:00."

"When can we go then?" Annie asked disappointedly.

"I'm not sure," Chris answered, "but I'll think of something."

"What about Mom?" Annie asked. "You know how she thinks that Granny's vision stuff is nonsense."

"Hmm," Chris said. "That is true. While I would never want to encourage you to lie to Mom or Dad, let's just not mention anything about this to either of them until I figure something out. Ok?"

Annie nodded her acceptance, but Jamie could see that she was not happy with her plan. She smiled to herself remembering that when she was thirteen, she had little patience and never wanted to wait for anything.

Chris then turned his attention to Jamie. "So, you still keep in close contact with your buckeye friends?"

"I haven't really kept up that much with them," she told him. "However, I received an email from one of the teachers I worked with in Grove City. Apparently, she has recently become engaged. There was a Zoom invite for this afternoon in the email, so I am thinking that she may be using this as a way to invite her friends to be in her wedding party."

"Cool," Annie said. "Will you do it?"

Jamie smiled at her young friend. "I would like to, but I will have to see the details of the wedding first. If it is somewhere in Ohio, I can probably manage it, but Lisa has rather extravagant tastes, and her parents are very well off. I think I remember hearing her mention that she would like to have a destination wedding, so that could be a problem for me."

"Like Hawaii?" Annie asked, excitedly. "That would be awesome."

Jamie laughed. "That would be expensive, and I couldn't take that much time off work."

"You could if it was in the summer," Annie pointed out.

Jamie shook her head. "The wedding date is already set for Valentine's Day."

"Oh, yeah. That would be a problem," Annie said.

"I guess I will find out later this afternoon," Jamie replied.

"Can you call me later tonight and let me know?" Annie asked. "I'm dying of curiosity."

"Oh yes, please do," Chris said with a grin. "We'll all sleep better tonight knowing Lisa's wedding plans."

Annie was quiet for a second and then said, "You don't have each other's numbers. Hang on a second." Then she picked up her phone and a few seconds later, both Chris and Jamie's phones pinged announcing a text message from Annie with shared contacts. Chris looked at his phone and then at Jamie. He grinned at her and rolled his eyes.

"All right then," he said. "Since we are all in communication now, I think we need to head home, before we waste the afternoon away."

Just as they were walking out, one of Annie's friends called and asked her to come over and help her with her geometry. Chris dropped her off and then drove Jamie home. He seemed anxious to get to his barn work, so she thanked him for taking her to brunch and then she quickly exited the truck and went into the house.

Later that afternoon, Jamie set up her laptop in her office work area and waited for the group call to begin. Part of her was excited about the idea of being involved in a wedding and part of her dreaded it. Weddings and the events that went with them could be fun, but there could be a lot involved too. Knowing Lisa there would be an engagement party, at least one shower, (probably more) a bachelorette party, which would probably involve at least a weekend, maybe longer. There would be dress selections and fittings. Then the wedding itself would involve a dinner and rehearsal the night before, and of course the wedding itself.

The more that she thought about the situation, the more concerns that she had. One of the first worries was the expense. Several trips to Ohio would cost her money. Hopefully, she could stay at Pam's house some of the time, but a bachelorette party could be pricey. Then there would be the dress, shoes, and hair, and make-up.

Finally, she admitted to herself what was really bothering her. It wasn't so much the money as it was the fact that she would be attending all the events dateless. She had been invited to a few weddings since she and Craig had broken up, but she had always been able to conveniently use her father's illness as an excuse not to attend. Unfortunately, that was no longer a viable option for her. The thought of going through all the wedding festivities alone was not appealing.

After a few more minutes of feeling sorry for herself, Jamie suddenly felt bad. This was a big moment for Lisa, and she should feel honored that she was included, especially since she had moved so far away. She told herself to knock off the pity party and at least listen to what she had to say with enthusiasm. Then she could make a rational decision after learning all the details.

At that very moment, the computer came to life and the Zoom call began. Once all seven girls were on the screen, Lisa began a speech that lasted for about fifteen minutes. She announced her engagement to her long-time boyfriend, Daryl, and stated the date as February 14th. After laughing about how she had always dreamed about having a destination wedding, she told them that Daryl had convinced her that it just wasn't practical for everyone in their families and the wedding party (Good for Daryl). Then she told them that the ceremony and reception would be held at Brenton Hall. Jamie was familiar with the name, and she knew that it was a very upscale venue.

At that point, she then officially invited them to be bridesmaids at her wedding. That was met with smiles and a round of applause from the girls. Lisa informed them that her sister, Laura, who was not able to be on the Zoom call that day, would be her maid of honor. She then went on to explain that she and Laura had devised a set of guidelines for the wedding party, to help make the preparations more organized and keep the events flowing smoothly. The guidelines were going to be emailed to all of them at 6:00.

Then Lisa asked them to read the document carefully and sign it if they were willing to fully participate by following all the guidelines. They needed to return the signed forms within one week, because if she needed to find any new bridesmaids, it could take some time. Then she thanked them for their time and ended the call.

Jamie stared at the now blank screen and was somewhat stunned. For some reason, she had the feeling that she had just finished a job interview. What could be the guidelines to be in a wedding party? You attended all the events, bought a dress and shoes, and showed up for the wedding.

Jamie then checked on her laundry before beginning to work on some schoolwork that she had brought home. She was so absorbed in her work that she lost track of the time. When she finally looked at her phone, it was 6:15. She stopped what she was doing and checked her computer. As promised, there was an email from Lisa. When she opened the attachment, it was two pages long. Jamie frowned and hit the print button.

Taking the papers to the living room, she curled up on the couch and began to read. The guidelines were numbered and double spaced.

#1 – The dresses and shoes have already been selected. You will need to make a fitting appointment with your nearest David's Bridal Salon and use my name. The dresses are $450. The shoes are $125. There are payment plan options available.

#2 – A hair stylist and make-up artist will be available the day of the wedding. The cost will be $50 each per person. Please don't arrive at the

wedding with a non- natural hair color. Also, I would like all of you to have your hair as close to shoulder length as possible. All hair and make-up must be approved by Laura or myself when finished.

#3 - There will be two wedding showers. One on December 14th, a lady's shower and one on Jan 15th which will be a couple's shower. All bridesmaids will be expected to attend both.

#4. The engagement party will be held on Oct 23rd at the Beechwood Garden Restaurant. Please RSVP if you are coming alone or with a date by Sept 30th.

#5 – The bachelorette party is a surprise destination but reserve the dates of Jan 20 – 23. Laura will be contacting you about the cost of your room and your share of the bride's room.

#6 – The rehearsal dinner will be held at the Brownhill Club on the 13th followed by a rehearsal at the venue. There   will be no plus 1's for the dinner, unless they are in the wedding party.

#7 – You may have a plus 1 at the wedding, but only if it is someone that Daryl and I have previously met and that we agree to have at our wedding.

#8 – We have blocked a number of rooms for the 13th and 14th of February at the Hyatt which is near the venue. You will need to make a reservation there by December 1st. We will be getting dressed and doing make-up in these rooms.

#9 – Please give careful consideration to all of these guidelines. We want all our wedding events to be smooth flowing and enjoyable for us and for our guests. If you do not feel that you can fully participate in all these events, please bow out and allow us the opportunity to find someone else who can.

Jamie sat dumbfounded for a few minutes. She never imagined that there would be that many events to commit to and that there would be so much expense involved. This was out of control. She did some quick math in her head, and calculated that with the dress, shoes, gifts for the showers and the engagement party, and the rooms at the Hyatt, it would cost her close to $2000, and that didn't include expenses for the bachelorette party. Never mind the expense of that, because after a quick glance at a calendar, she realized that it started on a Wednesday, so there was no way that she could take that much time off work unless she took it without pay, and with all these other expenses that was just not possible. Besides that, as a new employee she would not consider making that request.

It was very clear what she needed to do. There was no way that she could handle the commitment that was being asked by this bride. She picked up her phone and scrolled until she found Lisa's number. After taking a deep breath, she hit the call button. It only took one ring for her to answer.

"Hi, Jamie."

"Hi, Lisa. How are you?"

"I am fantastic," she replied. "How are things going up there in Wisconsin?"

"I am doing well. I really like my new job. I have a great class of 2nd graders and my year is off to a wonderful start. How is your school year going?"

"Oh, I took a year's leave of absence," Lisa told her. "Planning a wedding is a full-time job."

Jamie did not even know how to respond to that. She couldn't even imagine being able to take a year off work for any reason, much less to plan a wedding. Somehow that made what she had to say a little easier.

"I see," was her response and then she plunged right into what she had to say. "Lisa, I have read your list of guidelines and since I am so far away now, and I had to spend so much money on moving here, I don't think I will be able to be a part of your wedding party. I'm really sorry. I'm very flattered and touched that you have asked me, but it just wouldn't be fair for me to be a partial participant."

The silence on the other end of the line was somewhat concerning, but her eventual response was surprising.

"This is about Craig, isn't it?" Lisa asked.

"What does this have to do with Craig?" Jamie was totally surprised by this question.

"You don't want to be at the wedding because you know that he will be there. I think that is a terrible reason to back out. Don't you think it's time to grow up?"

Then Jamie remembered. Daryl and Craig were cousins. Naturally, he would be at the wedding. That, however, had nothing to do with her reasons for declining the invitation to be a bridesmaid.

"Lisa, that has nothing to do with it," she attempted to explain. "I simply can't afford the expense, and as a new employee, I can't take the time off work that I would need to I was to participate in all of the events in the wedding."

It was quiet again for a moment, and then there was another surprising statement. "He has been asking about you."

"Who? Craig?"

"Yes, he was asking where you went and why."

"That's none of his concern."

"I think he still might have feelings for you," Lisa told her. "He misses you."

"He should have thought of that before he lied to me and cheated on me," Jamie responded. "Did you tell him where I am?"

Another silent moment passed. "Daryl told him. They are family, you know. I'm sure he still has your number anyway."

"And I'm sure he is still blocked and if he attempts to call me from another number, it will be a waste of time. I've moved away and I have moved on." Jamie said emphatically. "Lisa, I wish you the very best of luck with your wedding and all of your events, and again I'm very sorry that I can't participate."

"Jamie..." Lisa began and then hesitated one more time and just at that moment there was a thud at the door.

She smiled and thought to herself, "Barney to the rescue."

"Lisa," Jamie said. "There is someone at my door. I've got to go. Again, I wish you and Daryl the best. Good-bye." Then she unceremoniously disconnected the call. A few seconds later, she opened the door and Barney bounded in.

"You are not supposed to be here, my friend," she said, "but your timing is perfect." Before closing the door, she looked towards the woods to see if Annie was following him. She didn't know if Annie had returned yet, but she had a suspicion that her young friend might have let her dog out and sent him this way just so that she could come and get him and find out about the wedding. After her conversation with Lisa, she really wasn't in the mood to discuss with Annie why she had chosen not to be involved in the wedding.

After a moment of thought, she picked up her phone and scrolled to the text message that Annie had sent her earlier. Then she sent a quick text to Chris.

"Barney is here."

A couple of minutes later, he called her.

"Damn that dog," he said. "I Just let him out. Maybe he thought Annie was there with you."

"Is she home yet?"

"No, Mom and Dad are coming through town at about eight and they are going to pick her up," he told her. "I have no idea where the whistle is, so I will come and get him."

Jamie started to say that he could stay until his parents passed by, but something stopped her. She did tell him that there was no hurry.

It was about ten minutes before she heard a knock at the door. After she opened the door, he stepped in and looked at Barney. "I wish I had an explanation for this," he said. "The dog thinks this is his second home."

Jamie laughed. "It's really not that big of a deal. I guess I could have brought him over to your place. To tell you the truth, at first, I thought maybe Annie was home, and she sent him over here, so she could get the scoop on the wedding."

Chris laughed. "I wouldn't have put that past her, but she isn't home yet." Then he looked at her for a moment and asked. "So did you get invited to be in the wedding party?"

Jamie nodded. "I certainly did, but I can't do it."

"It was a destination wedding?" he asked.

"Oh no," she said. Then she picked up the guideline page from the coffee table and handed it to him. It was getting dark, so she switched on the lamp and as he began to read, he sat down on the couch. Without even thinking, she sat down in the rocking chair and began to pet Barney, who was in his usual spot in front of it.

Eventually, Chris looked up from the paper. "Good Lord," he said. "Who are these people? They are certainly asking a lot of their friends."

"I calculated that it will be well over $2000," she told him.

"At least," he answered. "These are all high-end places."

She raised her eyebrows at him. He grinned. "I also went to *The Ohio State University.* I know the area well."

"Oh, I see. Then you understand that this whole wedding is going to be a giant money pit."

"So, you are going to say, '*No thank you*' to the bride?'

"I already did," she answered.

"Was she upset?"

Jamie thought for a few seconds and then she decided to tell him the whole story. "Lisa and I were never all that close, so I was a little surprised to be asked to be a bridesmaid. Then after our phone conversation just a little while ago, I realized that she may have had an ulterior motive."

"What would that be?" he asked.

"I completely forgot that her fiancé and my...uh...former boyfriend are cousins," she said. "She practically accused me of not wanting to be at the wedding because I knew that he would be there. I told her that I couldn't care less what he did, but I thanked her for thinking of me and wished her well. Then she began to plead his case and tell me how he missed me. I got a little agitated and told her he blew his chance with me, and I had moved on. I think she was going to argue with me some more, but Barney here arrived at that exact moment, and I blew her off and hung up."

Jamie then leaned down and nuzzled the dog. "You are a good boy, aren't you? Aren't you? Yes, you are. Yes, you are."

When she looked up, Chris was staring at her intently. "He cheated on you, didn't he?"

"Yes, he did," she told him. "When I found out, I kicked his ass to the curb and never looked back."

"Good for you," he said. "I'm curious. How did you find out?"

Jamie sighed. "A friend of mine saw him in a restaurant with another woman, and they were acting quite cozy."

"And she reported this back to you?" he asked. Jamie nodded.

"Did you believe her?"

"No," she answered. "Not at first. I was so young and stupid, but she had the foresight to video them with her phone and put a time and date stamp on it. When she showed it to me, I had no choice but to believe it. He was supposed to be playing in a golf league, which it turns out that he never signed up for. He tried to deny it, but when I showed him the video, there was nothing he could say. I told him I never wanted to see him again and threw him out of my life."

"Is that part of the reason that you applied for a job here?" he wanted to know.

"That and the fact that my father died after a long illness, and then my mother fled to Florida, so I felt like I needed a new start," she said. "I like it here. I enjoy the work and I'm making new friends." She picked up the wedding guidelines that he had set down on the coffee table. "After my conversation with Lisa, I could see that it was going to stir up a lot of old drama. I don't need that in my life."

"Good for you," he said.

It was quiet for a moment and then Jamie said, "How did you find out that you were being cheated on?" She waited for him to ask how she knew about the details of his broken relationship, but he didn't.

"Cassie came to me and told me that she had found someone else," he said. "She told me that she didn't think that she ever loved me and that she wished my next woman all the luck in the world because she would need it. Then she was gone. Six months later, she came crawling back, saying that she had made a mistake. I uh...as you so aptly put it, kicked her to the curb. A few weeks later, she moved to New York with a musician. That was three years ago. I haven't heard from her since."

"Wow, it seems as if we have something in common," she told him.

"It does seem so," he agreed.

"Let me ask you something," Jamie said. "Do you sometimes wish people would stop feeling sorry for you and leave you alone about ...dating?"

"Yes," he replied. "If I want to go out with a girl, I am perfectly capable of finding one myself. I don't need any help. Are people here trying to fix you up?"

"Not yet," she answered, "but to tell you the truth, you are the first person that I have told my sad story to." She paused a moment and then continued. "It's hard to talk about, isn't it?"

"It is. Why did you decide to tell me?"

"I guess maybe I felt like you would understand," she said.

"I do," he answered, "and don't worry; your story will stay with me."

"I appreciate that," she told him.

At that very moment, Barney suddenly sat up and barked as he looked toward the kitchen. Then he stood up and walked in there and stood in front of the refrigerator. The two of them followed him and then Chris said, "No boy, you are not begging for any ice cream here. You will have to wait until you get home, which we should probably be doing. Let's go."

When they walked back to the living room, they both stopped and stared at the chair because it was rocking as if it had just been pushed. "I must have caused that when I got up," she said. At that moment, a cool breeze came through the open window.

"It was probably the wind," he said.

Jamie shivered a little bit. "It is getting a little cool outside."

Chris walked over to the window and closed it for her.

"Thank you," she told him.

As Barney settled back in his favorite spot, the two of them stared silently at the chair for a moment. "I don't know whether to be fascinated by this chair or to be afraid of it," Jamie said to him.

"Because it rocked a little," he asked her.

"Well, it's not just that," she said. Then she went on to tell him about the tie coming undone and the chair moving on its own. This had now happened about three times. "I keep telling myself that it is my imagination," she told him, "but now I'm not so sure."

Chris gave her a look that she wasn't sure how to interpret. "Are you trying to tell me that you believe in ghosts?" he asked.

"I don't know," Jamie said. "I never gave the idea much thought before now."

He was quiet for a moment and then presented her with an idea. "Let's approach this from a logical point of view. At least to start. Do you have any masking tape, or maybe electrical tape?"

She laughed. "I'm a teacher. I have all kinds of tape." She then went into her workroom and returned shortly with a roll of masking tape.

Chris tore off four short strips of tape and placed two on each side of the bottom part of the chair. Then he tore four more strips of tape and placed them on the floor directly correlating to the strips on the chair.

He looked up at her and said, "Be very careful not to move the chair and you can see if it moves on its own."

She smiled and nodded. "That's a good idea. Thank you."

Chris laughed. "If it does move on its own, we'll have Annie and her friends over along with Granny and have a séance." he answered. "If you ever need anything, don't hesitate to call us. We are close by. Oh, by the way, we always make a party out of watching the Ohio State football games. You should come by next Saturday. I'm not sure of the time. I'll tell Mom to let you know."

"That sounds like fun," she said.

"All right Barney let's go," he told the dog. "We'll get some ice cream at home." Once again, at the mention of his favorite treat, Barney was running for the truck.

"Good night," Chris said with a chuckle, and then he was out the door.

Jamie locked it behind him and sat on the couch and watched him leave. She stayed there for a little while as she contemplated all the events of the day and then decided she would put it all out of her mind. She picked up the remote and began to search for some mindless television to watch.

Chapter Five

The next morning, she checked the chair, and it didn't appear to have moved at all, and she began to wonder if maybe she had gotten carried away with her imagination. As she drove to school, she thought about Chris's invitation to come to their house to watch the football game the following Saturday. It sounded like fun, but was he really serious, or was it just a thought, and would he remember to mention it to his mother?

Jamie didn't see much of Mary that day because she apparently was still quite busy. Kim was out with a sick child and Gina was having lunch with some students, so Leslie and Jamie ate alone. When she was asked about her weekend, Jamie told her about doing crafts and baking with Annie. Then she went on to mention the problem with her chair, and Chris's suggestion.

Leslie gave her an interesting look, and then said that she thought that was good thinking because the idea of a ghost moving the chair was not very likely. Besides that, the chair had belonged to Carol's grandmother, Maggie, and she was still alive. Then, in typical Leslie fashion, she suddenly did a one hundred eighty degree turn in her thinking.

"I almost forgot," she said.

"Forgot what?" Jamie asked.

"Remember when I told you that I might know who bought that chair?"

"Yes, I do, but you never said anymore about it," Jamie told her.

Leslie looked at her watch and sighed. "It's about time to go, but I think maybe after school, you and I are going to do a little investigating."

Jamie gathered up her lunch things and stood up. "That sounds interesting. I'm in."

Once the buses were gone at the end of the day, Leslie turned to her and said, "Follow me."

Leslie then led her down a hall and around a corner. She stopped at a doorway at the end of the hall. Jamie knew that it was the room of Bessie Walker, the remedial reading teacher that Carol had told her about not long after she had moved here. She had only had a few encounters with the woman. Just as Carol had told her, Bessie kept mostly to herself, eating alone in her room, and leaving almost immediately after school was out on most days. The door was open, and Bessie was putting papers in her school bag, preparing to go home. She was a woman who appeared to be in her fifties. Her hair was gray and cut in a short practical manner. She was wearing a pair of blue polyester pants and a white polo shirt.

"Hi Bessie," Leslie said in a friendly way. "Do you have a minute? There is something I wanted to ask you about."

The woman looked up at Leslie and then glanced over at Jamie. "I guess so," she answered. "What's on your mind?"

"You have met Jamie Barnes, our new second grade teacher, haven't you?" Leslie asked.

At this point, Bessie did let out a small smile. "I'm not sure that we have been formally introduced, but I am aware of who she is. I have heard some good things about her."

This surprised and pleased Jamie, but before she could respond, Leslie jumped in and began the conversation about the chair. She told Bessie about how Jamie was living in Carol's grandmother's house and how she had come to buy a chair from Velma at her store. Bessie listened intently as Leslie continued the story all the way up to the point where Annie thought that it was the same chair and how Carol had explained that the chair had been sold at a yard sale by accident.

"That is a very interesting story," Bessie said. "but what do you want to know from me?"

"Well," Bessie said. "when Jamie was telling me about the chair, something jogged in my memory about either Brenda or Dora buying a chair, possibly at the yard sale at Carol's grandmother's house. Do you remember anything about that?"

Bessie looked back and forth between the two of them for a moment, and then she spoke. "Yes, Brenda did buy a rocking chair at that sale. I remember this distinctly because it was a lovely wooden chair, and she insisted on painting it white so it would match the other furniture in her back room. Dora and I were horrified, but she did it anyway."

Jamie and Leslie exchanged a look. "I guess that settles it. It is the same chair," Leslie said. Then she turned back to Bessie. "I suppose it was sold with all of Brenda's other furniture after she died."

Bessie shook her head. "No, Brenda sold it about three months after she bought it."

"Why?" Jamie and Leslie both asked at the same time.

Bessie shrugged. "I have no idea. One day the chair was gone and when Dora and I asked her about it, she just said that she had decided that she didn't like it anymore. Then she said something about how she should never have painted it, and that it was Velma's problem now. That was all she would say about it." Bessie looked at Jamie. "So, what possessed you to buy a painted wooden chair?"

"I don't really know," Jamie told her. "I needed a chair, and I decided to check out Velma's store. It was shoved way in the back corner, and it was covered with stuffed animals, but for some reason it appealed to me. I guess you could say that I bought it on a whim."

"Does a white chair fit into your décor?" Bessie asked.

"Oh no," Jamie told her. "I had it restored at the hardware store."

"Earl?"

Jamie nodded and laughed. "Please don't tell me he's related to you. I seem to hear that a lot around here."

"No," Bessie said. "Earl and I are not related. We ...uh...kind of dated in high school."

With that statement, a silence descended on the room. Jamie could tell by the look on Leslie's face that she couldn't have been more surprised.

Then Bessie suddenly changed the subject. "So, are you enjoying the chair?"

Jamie thought that was a bit of a strange question, but she tried to answer it truthfully. "Yes, I enjoy rocking in it. It's very peaceful. I've even fallen asleep in it a couple of times."

Bessie picked up her bag and hung it on her shoulder. "Well, I am glad to hear that the chair has found its way back home. I'm sure that it's happier there. Now I hate to be rude, but I have to take my cat to the vet's office before it closes."

Leslie then spoke up. "We will get out of your way then. Thank you though for clearing up that mystery for us."

"I'm glad I could help," Bessie answered. Then she looked at Jamie. "It was nice to finally meet you."

"Nice meeting you too," Jamie said.

When they reached their own hallway, the two of them stopped outside of their doors. "Did you find anything she said strange?" Leslie asked.

Jamie thought for a moment before she replied. "Do you mean when she said that maybe the chair is happier now?"

"Yes," Leslie answered. "Somehow, I think that she only told us part of the story."

Jamie looked at her friend. "I think maybe you are right."

The next day Mary did make a point of finding Jamie and inviting her to their Ohio State party on Saturday. She asked if she could bring anything, and Mary told her just to bring some kind of finger food.

On Wednesday afternoon, the weather turned unusually cold, and it began to rain, and continued through Thursday afternoon. Jamie needed some groceries, so when there seemed to be a break in the downpour right after school, she headed straight to the Walmart in Valene. When she entered the store, there was only a slight drizzle coming down. Unfortunately, when she came out, the hard rain had returned, and she had left her umbrella in the car. She sighed and decided that she needed to bite the bullet and just get wet.

By the time that she got home, and had unloaded and put away her purchases, she was ready for a hot shower. When she finished, she put her hair up in a towel, and threw on a pair of sweatpants and a sweatshirt, because there seemed to be a chill in the house. Then she went to the kitchen to see about dinner. Staring into the refrigerator, she spotted the tuna casserole that she had made the night before. Just as she put the dish into the microwave and set the timer, she heard a knock at the door. Puzzled, she went and looked through the window and was surprised to see that it was Chris.

When she opened the door, she stepped aside to let him in. "Hi," she said. "Come on in. It's nasty out there, isn't it?"

"It sure is," he answered and then looked around. "Where is he?"

"Where is who?" she asked.

"Barney," he said.

Jamie was confused. "Barney isn't here."

Now Chris was the one who was baffled. "Mom texted me and said that Barney was here and asked me to get him on my way home from the feed store." Then he quickly placed a call to his mother and asked her to clarify. He listened for a moment and then ended the call.

"I'm sorry," he said. "Annie told Mom that Barney had taken off and was probably here, but he apparently showed up and Annie forgot to mention it to her. I guess I caught you just out of the shower or something."

Jamie's face then turned red, and she looked down to see if she had only thought that she had gotten dressed. Then she saw him glance at her head, and she remembered the towel that she had wrapped around her hair.

"Oh yeah, I got soaked coming out of Walmart," she told him. "I do have something to tell you though if you got a few minutes. I learned something interesting about the chair."

"Did you now?" he asked.

Jamie put her hand up to the towel on her head. "Can you just give me a few minutes?"

"Sure," he said with a smile. "If you have a good story, I can wait."

Jamie hurried to the bathroom and quickly semi-dried her hair. When she returned, she found Chris in the kitchen.

"I heard your microwave going off," he told her. "I took the dish out and put it on the counter. "It smells delicious."

"It's tuna casserole that I made last night," she said. "I was reheating it for my dinner. Would you like to join me?"

Chris hesitated for just a few seconds. "I love tuna, and Mom and Dad hate it, so I rarely get any, so I think maybe I will join you."

"Good," Jamie answered. "Iced tea?"

"That would be great," he said.

Five minutes later, the two of them were enjoying the casserole and Jamie began to tell him the story that Bessie had told her and Leslie. When she finished, he stopped eating and looked at her. "That's an odd thing to say."

"That's what we thought," she told him.

"Did you take that to mean that the chair did weird things in Brenda's house too?" he asked.

Jamie shrugged. "I guess that you could take it that way, or maybe she just meant that it was nice that the chair had been restored and returned to its original house."

"Maybe she did," he answered. "By the way, have you checked the tape on the chair?"

"It hadn't moved as of last night, but I was running late this morning and then with the rain and everything this evening, I haven't checked it today," she said.

Chris took the last bite off the plate and wiped his mouth with a napkin. "Let's look at it," he suggested.

The two of them went into the living room and then kneeled down and inspected the tape marks on the floor. "It doesn't appear to have moved at all," Chris said. "Have you sat in it this week?"

Jamie shook her head. "No, I intentionally didn't sit there so I wouldn't mess up our experiment."

"Well, I did come up with a plan to ask Granny what she meant with her little statement about the chair," Chris told her.

"Oh really. What's that?" Jamie asked.

"When we have Saturday afternoon game parties, Mom arranges to pick up Granny's groceries on Friday evening," Chris said, "so I volunteered to take care of it for her. It was no problem; she was all over that. I can swing by and pick you up on the way. We can get the groceries and take them to her apartment. Then we will have a chance to talk to her."

"What about Annie?" Jamie wanted to know.

"Oh, she usually stays with her friend Lacey on Friday nights," he answered. "I'm not going to mention anything to her. Annie tends to get a little dramatic, and I think Granny will be more apt to open up to us without her."

"Won't she be upset?"

"She might, but she will get over it," he told her with a laugh. "With thirteen-year-old girls, they are always carrying on about something."

Jamie smiled. "Yes, I suppose that is true."

"What time will you be home from school tomorrow?" he asked her.

After thinking for a moment, she replied to his question. "I'll probably be home no later than 4:30."

"All right. I'll pick you up around 5 then," he said.

"I'll be ready." she told him. "Am I not supposed to mention this to your mom?"

"It would probably be for the best," he told her.

Something about this bothered Jamie, but she was looking forward to this little adventure, so she didn't say anything.

Chris then moved toward the door and opened it. "Thanks for dinner," he said. "I'll see you tomorrow."

"Thanks for the company," she answered. "Good night."

The rain had stopped by the next morning, but it was still cool and gloomy. It was Friday dress down day, so Jamie wore jeans and a sweater that she had dug out of her winter clothes. While she was checking herself in the mirror, she debated about whether she should consider changing the sweater and saving it for her evening out. Then she realized what she was doing and reminded herself that this was *not* a date. After another

127

moment of thought she wore the sweater to school, deciding if it was still not fresh when she got home, she could change it. It was only a trip to the store and then a quick visit with Chris's grandmother.

As Friday's often did, the day seemed to drag on and on. There were an endless number of small problems that had to be dealt with. It was too cool and wet to go out on the playground, so the after-lunch recess had to be held in the room. It was the third day in a row in which the children weren't able to go outside, and they were definitely showing signs of cabin fever. After an endless amount of tattling and bickering, Jamie ended recess a little early, and assigned them to work in their chrome books.

An hour later, she sent them to art class, and sat down to enjoy the quiet. She pulled her phone out of the desk drawer to check her messages. There were two. One was from her mother. She had little to say, but she sent a multitude of pictures showing her partying on the beach with her friends. Jamie didn't even bother to respond.

The other message was from Chris. Jamie felt her breath catch because she hoped that he wasn't cancelling. That was not the case, at all.

"Hi Jamie. I was just thinking that after we finish with Granny, we could go grab a bite to eat. I know this restaurant in Valene that serves great steaks and seafood. I thought maybe we could discuss whatever pearls of wisdom Granny gives us over dinner. Let me know what you think, or we can talk about it when I come to pick you up."

Without thinking, Jamie responded to his message.

"Sounds great. See you at 5."

The day finally ended and as the last bus drove off, Jamie let out a sigh of relief. As she and Leslie walked back to their rooms, her friend expressed Jamie's exact thoughts.

"TGIF. The rain and kids have just about driven me right up the wall the last couple of days. I can't wait to get on the road to Milwaukee."

"I know," Jamie agreed. "I'm ready for the weekend too."

"Do you have big plans?" Leslie wanted to know.

"I'm going to the Wilson's tomorrow for their Ohio State football party," Jamie said, being careful not to mention her plans for the evening. Leslie was a good friend, but she tended to be a little excitable about things and Jamie didn't want her reading too much into a simple friendship.

"I guess that could be fun if you are a buckeye fan," she laughed. "Michigan doesn't play this weekend, so I'm not sure what Joe and I are going to do."

They had reached their rooms, so Jamie simply said, "I'm sure it will be fun whatever you do. Enjoy, and get some rest."

"Will do," Leslie said, and she went into her room.

Jamie gathered her things, but decided to wait until Leslie was gone, before leaving, because she didn't want to appear in a rush to get home. She sighed to herself, thinking that this evening certainly did involve a lot of secrecy.

Ten minutes later, Leslie stuck her head in the door and said, "Bye. Have a good one."

"You too," Jamie answered. She waited just a couple of minutes and then looked out the window. She saw Leslie's car leaving and Mary just getting into hers. The coast was clear. Five minutes later, she was on her way home also.

Back at home in her bedroom, she looked at herself in the mirror again. After a little thought, she changed into a dark green sweater and reapplied her make-up. She told herself that she wasn't dressing for a date; it was just refreshing to wear something nice and to have her make-up look good.

Chris arrived right at 5:00 and the two of them were soon on their way. Jamie looked over at him with a smile and asked him if either his mother or Annie had questioned anything about him volunteering to take care of Granny's errands.

"No," he answered. "Mom's head is all into getting ready for tomorrow and Annie went home with Lacey on the bus. I think there is some big dance thing next weekend at their school, and they were all into who liked who and who would ask who to dance. You know; all that middle school drama."

Jamie laughed. "It's been a while, but I remember well. Drama was a way of life. I think kids that age feed off it."

"Yes, they do," he answered. "High school was better, but there was still a lot of foolishness."

"As opposed to the grown-up world?" she asked with a little giggle.

He looked over at her. "In the grown-up world, I can have more control over my life."

"I suppose," she said, "but you are fortunate to work in a family situation, where you have more control than someone who works for an outside employer."

Chris sighed. "Working in a family business has advantages, as well as disadvantages. Granted that I don't have to put up with a lot of bureaucratic stuff, but at this point, I'm still working for my father. It's good most of the time, but we don't always see eye to eye all the time."

"I'm guessing you have ideas about how to change things and he wants to stick with the old ways?"

He grinned over at her. "That was a very intuitive thought, and you are correct. However, a couple of years ago, I did convince him to cash rent out all our corn fields. It is much less work, and actually more profitable. Now we just deal with the cows and a few goats. Dad is content with things as they are, but I have my eye on a farm down the road. I think it may be coming up for sale soon. I guess if it does, we'll see."

After a minute, he asked her a question. "Something tells me that maybe you and your mother aren't so close?"

"You are also intuitive," she said. "We were never extremely close, but we got along all right. Then after my father died, she just sort of flipped out. She moved to Sarasota, Florida, and she is living what she thinks is her dream life with all her party friends."

"Are you an only child?"

"I am, so now I feel like I'm kind of alone in the world. That's why I really appreciate the kindness that your family has shown me. Even before Dad died, we never had much of a family life. They were both kind of closed people and to be honest, they didn't really get along all that well. So, during the holidays and special events, we just sort of went through the motions."

"That's too bad," he said. "As a family, we have certainly had our moments, but we have always gotten through them and continued to be there for each other."

"It shows," Jamie said. "I have sensed the togetherness when I have been around you all."

At that point they had arrived in the pick-up area of the grocery store. Chris checked in on his phone and a short time later, the attendant brought out the order. There weren't too many bags, so they were able to get all of them in the back seat of the truck.

A short time later, Chris parked his truck in front of Nora's apartment, which was located right in the center of the senior complex. Once she was inside of Nora's little home, Jamie was impressed. There was a small living area, and directly behind that there was a galley kitchen and a small table with two chairs. There were two open doors off the living room. One room was a bathroom and the other was a bedroom. The apartment was very clean, and she assumed that people from the center cleaned it.

Chris carried the groceries to the kitchen area and began to put them away. He seemed to know where everything went, so Jamie decided to sit down and talk to Nora who was sitting in the recliner, which appeared to be one of those electric ones that rose up.

"I didn't know that Chris was bringing you with him," Nora said with a smile. "This is a pleasant surprise. Are you two young people going out tonight?"

Jamie wasn't sure exactly how to respond to her question, but Chris quickly intervened. "Well, Granny, the truth is that Jamie and I have something that we wanted to ask you about."

"What is that dear?" she asked.

"Give me two seconds here," he answered. When he had finished putting things away, he came and sat next to Jamie on the couch. The two of them looked at each other, and Jamie decided that it was her question, so she spoke first.

"Do you remember when you were leaving Annie's birthday party a couple of weeks ago? You said something to me that I didn't quite understand."

Nora stared at her for a moment, and then it was as if she suddenly remembered what she said. "Oh, do you mean about taking care of the chair?"

"Yes," Jamie replied. "What exactly did you mean by that?"

Nora stared at her for a moment and Jamie had a strange feeling that she was listening to something that neither she nor Chris could hear. Then she closed her eyes and then after a moment, she spoke quietly. "You have done well by finding the chair and getting it restored. Now you just need to make sure that it stays in good condition."

A chill went through Jamie. There were several questions that went through her mind...how?...why?...who? Chris, however, got right to the point.

"Granny, who are you talking to about the chair?"

Nora turned and smiled at him. "I don't think that I am supposed to say, but it doesn't matter."

Then she turned back to Jamie. "There is nothing to be afraid of. You came here as part of a plan. You just haven't figured that out yet. It will all become clear in time. Just be patient. The chair is just the connection to the whole plan. Don't be concerned by what it does. Just let it do its thing. That's really all I have to say." Then she closed her eyes for a few seconds.

When she opened them, she smiled. "My nighttime girl will be in here shortly to help me with my dinner and to get me ready for bed. Now you two need to run and have a nice evening," she said.

Jamie was at a complete loss for words, but apparently, Chris was used to these strange comments from his grandmother, because he stood and went to her, giving her a kiss on the cheek. "All right. Thank you, Granny. We'll get out of your way."

Not knowing what else to do, Jamie stood up and smiled at the woman. "It was good to see you again, Nora."

"Everyone calls me Granny," she said. "You should too."

This small thing made Jamie feel warm all over. "All right, I will. Good night, Granny."

Just as they were about to go out the door, Granny called out after them. "Don't worry I won't say anything to Jake or Mary."

The drive to the restaurant was quiet. Both Chris and Mary were attempting to process Granny's words. Once inside, Jamie attempted to pull herself together. She smiled at Chris.

"This is a nice place. Thank you for bringing me here," she said, as she looked over the menu. "Do you have any suggestions?"

"If you are looking for seafood, I would go with the grilled shrimp skewers, or the shrimp alfredo," he told her. "If you want steak then maybe the steak tacos."

"You know the menu well," she answered.

"I haven't been here much lately," he said. "It's not really the kind of place that you eat at alone."

Jamie smiled at him, knowing exactly what he meant. "I hear that," she said.

The waiter then came to take their order. When he was gone, Jamie looked at him and asked, "What was your take on what Granny said?"

"I'm not sure," he answered. "I've seen her do that thing where she closes her eyes before, and it is kind of ..."

"Creepy?"

"Yes," he replied. "It's kind of like she is listening to something."

"Or someone?"

"I think so," he said.

"Do you have any ideas about who that might be?" she wanted to know.

"I think there are several possibilities," he said.

"Should we be logical again and just make a list?" Jamie suggested.

"That might be a good idea," Chris answered.

The waiter then arrived with their salads and for a few minutes they were consumed with the business of eating. While they were eating, the subject of Granny was shelved, and Chris asked her about her days at OSU. They realized that since he was two years older than her, and she did her first two years mostly online, they were only actually on campus at the same time for a couple of semesters. They did, however, frequent some of the same places, and they laughed about the possibility that they could have crossed paths or even met years earlier.

When they had finished their dinner, they made their way to his truck, just before the skies opened and there was a massive downpour of rain. Chris had to drive back to Riley very slowly. Their plan was to go into Jamie's house and write down a list of people that Granny could be communicating with. Once they arrived in her driveway, the rain was coming down even harder and they debated about whether to run for the door or try to wait it out. Chris suggested that they wait ten minutes and then go for it.

While they waited, Jamie thought that Chris looked as if there was something on his mind. Then she thought that maybe her imagination was working overtime again.

When the ten minutes was up, the rain had let up a little, but not much. They both laughed and decided that they weren't going to melt. On the count of three, they both opened their doors and took off for the front porch. Chris made it to her front door very quickly, but Jamie didn't fare so well. Just after she stepped out of the truck, she swung at the door of the truck to close it, causing herself to lose her balance, and she ended up sitting in an enormous pool of water.

At first, she was somewhat stunned, but then as the rain pelted down on her, she realized that she couldn't just sit there, so she jumped and ran onto the porch. When she got there, she could tell Chris was trying not to laugh, so she just began to laugh at herself, and he soon joined in with her.

After a moment, she pulled her key out of her pocket and let them in. Inside the room, she flipped on the light and they both looked at each other and laughed some more. Then she went down the hall and returned with a towel which she handed to Chris. Jamie, however, was thoroughly drenched, so she went to her room to change her clothes. As she quickly ran her hairdryer through her hair, it occurred to her that this was an instant replay of the night before.

When she returned to the living room, she found Chris staring at the chair.

"What?" she asked.

He didn't say a word but pointed at it. Jamie looked where he was pointing and gasped. The chair was pushed all the way back to the wall.

Chapter Six

Jamie looked at Chris and said, "Please tell me that you moved the chair, just for a laugh."

After a few seconds, he grinned. "I did. I just wanted to see your reaction, and you didn't disappoint. The look on your face was priceless." When Jamie just stared at him without responding, he continued. "I'm sorry. Maybe I shouldn't have done that. You're not going to throw me out now, are you?"

Jamie really wanted to be upset with him, but somehow, she just couldn't. "No, I'm not going to throw you out. You are the only ally I've got in this crazy chair business. Come on, let's work on this list."

The two of them then went into the kitchen and Jamie pulled a pad of paper and a pen out of a drawer. "By the way, will your mother wonder why you are late getting back from Granny's?"

"Well, first of all, I am twenty-seven years old, and I don't need to answer to my mother which is a fact that I established when I moved out of the house and into the apartment over the garage. Secondly, I dropped a hint that I might stop by Eddie's after I finished with Granny."

"Eddie?"

"He's a buddy of mine that lives in Valene. I hang out with him from time to time," he explained.

"I see," she replied. "So, you did what you told Annie not to do."

"What was that?" he asked.

"The thing about lying?"

"I didn't lie," he said. "I just told her I might drop in there. We could have gone there, we just didn't."

"Hmmm."

"Anyway, Mom always goes to bed early." He looked at his watch. "She is probably reading in bed as we speak. Let's get on with this list. Shall we?"

"All right," she answered. "Who are our suspects?"

"As far as this house is concerned, we can't put Carol's grandmother down because she is still alive."

"But her mother has passed away," Jamie reminded him. "She picked up the pen and thought for a moment. "I'm not sure of her name."

"I think it was Liz...uh... Patterson," he told her.

Jamie wrote her name down and looked up.

"What about the teacher that bought the chair at the yard sale? And her friend?" he asked. "Didn't they die together in a car accident?"

"Yes," she answered, and added their names to the list.

They were both quiet for a moment as if they were searching for other ideas. Jamie finally mentioned the thought that was floating around in her head.

"I suppose we should add my father's name to the list," she said. "Granny did say that I came here as part of a plan. Maybe he somehow...." Then she wondered if she was reaching too much."

"I think we should include anybody that was close to either you or the situation," he added. "Which brings me to another thought."

"Your grandfather?" she asked. "Granny's husband? Maybe she talks to him a lot."

Chris shook his head. "I don't think so. He died when I was about two. Granny rarely talks about him. There is someone else though."

"Who is that?" she wanted to know.

"My brother, Kyle."

Jamie couldn't have been more stunned. "You have a brother who died?"

Chris nodded. "He was three and a half years older than me."

"I'm so sorry," Jamie said in a near whisper. "What happened to him?"

"He was killed in a tractor accident on the farm," he told her. "It was springtime, and he was trying to get the last of the corn planted and he was going too fast. The tractor overturned and pinned him underneath. He suffered massive brain injuries. He lived on a ventilator for a few days, but Mom and Dad had to make the decision to turn it off."

Now Jamie was speechless, and a tear rolled down her cheek as she could see the pain on his face. After a moment, she asked him a question. "I'm guessing that Annie doesn't remember him."

Chris shook his head. "She wasn't even a year old," he said. "Part of the reason I think that he should go on the list is that he was the apple of Granny's eye. They were very close. I could imagine that if it was possible, he would be talking to Granny."

"Do you think that he was the one telling Granny about Cassie?"

"I think it's highly possible," he answered. "Kyle always looked out for me. He took the big brother role very seriously."

"I see your point," Jamie said, "but he didn't have a connection to this house, did he?"

Chris shook his head. "No, he didn't, but Annie does. She has always loved being here. Carol's grandmother, Maggie, used to babysit for Annie when she was little. Then when Ellen rented the place, Annie would always follow Barney over here."

"I'm guessing that Kyle would probably feel protective of his little sister too?"

Chris did not immediately respond to her question. It seemed as if he was debating about what to say next. Eventually, he did answer her.

"It's more than that," he said quietly. "Kyle was not Annie's brother. He was her father."

"Her father? How was…"

"Kyle's high school girlfriend became pregnant in their senior year. Her family was very upset, of course. They were insistent that the baby be put up for adoption. Kyle wouldn't hear of it, and with Mom and Dad's support, he obtained full custody of her after she was born. Two months later, the girl's family moved to Arizona without even looking back. After Kyle died, Mom decided that the right thing to do was to inform Annie's mother of his death. The response from Holly and her parents was that it was not their problem, and they threatened Mom with a restraining order if she ever attempted to contact them again. So, they have raised her as their own."

Jamie was now completely overwhelmed with information overload. "Poor Annie," was all she could say.

Chris stared down at the table for a few seconds and then looked up at her. "Annie doesn't know. She was so little that she doesn't remember him. As far as she is concerned, Kyle was her older brother who died when she was a baby."

"Chris..."

"I know," he said. "Mom and I have gone round and round about this. I keep telling her that one day she is going to find out. A lot of people around Riley know about it. I worry that one of her friends will find out and spill the beans or maybe some mean girl will tell her out of viciousness."

"Oh, that would be horrible," Jamie said.

"I know, but I think that Mom thinks that the longer it goes on, the harder it will be to tell her," Chris answered. "Truthfully, I think that the reality is that Mom just has no idea how to go about it, so she just avoids the whole thing."

"What about your father?" Jamie asked.

Chris just shook his head. "Ever since Kyle died, Dad has just buried his feelings. He wants no controversy, so he just goes along with whatever Mom says."

"And you are caught in the middle of the whole thing?" she asked.

"For sure," he answered.

Jamie thought for a moment and then said, "I think maybe Kyle needs to go to the top of the list."

"I would agree with that," he answered.

"I had another idea," she told him.

"What is that?"

"I think maybe I should research into the history of the house," she said. "I don't want to ask Carol because ...."

"I know," he agreed. "The further we get into this, the stranger it gets."

"Right," she said. "For the time being, we will just keep it between the two of us."

Chris looked at his watch and then spoke. "It's getting late. I should be going."

The two of them stood up and walked to the front door. There was an awkward moment and then Jamie spoke.

"It's been quite an evening," she began. "About what you shared with me; you don't need to worry about me discussing it with anyone else."

He laughed. "I can't believe that Leslie didn't tell you."

Jamie shook her head. "I do remember her saying something about Annie being a surprise, but I didn't think much about it. That seemed obvious."

He looked at her for another minute and then asked her a question. "What has Leslie said about me?"

Jamie knew that her face was turning red. "Come on tell me," he said. "I don't care. I know Leslie well enough to know that she speaks her mind."

"She said that you were an ass."

Chris laughed out loud. "That doesn't surprise me."

"Well, she said that you were popular in high school and a pretty nice guy, but after your breakup with Cassie, you became kind of bitter and stuck up."

He thought for a moment. "I would say she hit the nail right on the head."

"You have never struck me as an ass or bitter and stuck up," Jamie said. "You have been very nice to me."

Chris smiled at her. "Maybe that's because you have been nice to me." Then he pulled open the door. "It looks like the rain has stopped."

"I guess I'll see you tomorrow," she said. "Thank you for dinner. I enjoyed it."

"I did too," he answered. "Maybe we should do it again sometime."

Jamie smiled. "I would like that."

"Good night," he answered and then he turned and walked to his truck.

Jamie stood at the door for a moment, trying to decide if he had just asked her out on a date. Then she began to think about how she would feel about it if he was asking her out. A warm feeling began to spread through her, but at the same time somewhere in her mind or maybe her heart, there were warning bells going off.

The next day Jamie headed to the Wilson home with her sweet pumpkin dip and ginger snap cookies. She was partly excited about the event and a little nervous about the fact that she had spent the entire evening before with Chris and no one was supposed to know. It seemed a little dishonest.

The party was fun. A few of the Wilson's friends were there, along with two of Mary's

153

sisters and their husbands. The food was placed on the dining room table so that everyone could help themselves as they wished. There was a large screen TV in the main living area and the room was filled with Ohio State fans. It was quite exciting, and everyone was very much into cheering the Buckeyes on.

Chris seemed to be in a good mood, and he didn't pay any more attention to her than he did to any of the other guests. Jamie then told herself that she had imagined him showing interest in her the night before. It was just a friend thing.

What she did notice was that Annie was unusually quiet. She sat with the group, but something just seemed off with the girl. At halftime, everyone went to the table and reloaded their plates. Jamie noticed Annie heading toward the stairs, so she followed her and stopped her just as she got to the bottom of the steps.

"Hey Annie," she said. "I noticed that you are kind of quiet today. Are you feeling all right?"

"I'm just tired." she said. "I didn't get much sleep last night." She turned to start up the steps, but then for some reason, she changed her mind and turned back to Jamie. "Lacey and I probably aren't going to be friends anymore."

"That's too bad," Jamie said. "Why not?"

Annie sighed. "Lacey wants to be a cheerleader. She is going out for this new sixth grade squad that the school is starting."

"And you are not interested in cheerleading?" Jamie asked.

"No," Annie answered. "I think standing on the sideline dancing and chanting is silly. Most of the cheerleaders I've ever seen are stuck up and mostly concerned with looking pretty."

"I see, and I guess you expressed your opinion to Lacey?"

"I did, and then we had this big fight," Annie told her. "She ended up going downstairs and sleeping on the couch. This morning she was still mad, and she wasn't speaking to me."

"That's too bad," Jamie said. "I know that Lacey is your best friend. These things happen sometimes though. Maybe it will work out."

"That is what Mom said," Annie answered, "but she told me that I should support Lacey in cheerleading if that is what she wants to do. Then she said that I need to apologize to Lacey, and I probably should, but she said nasty things to me too."

Jamie smiled at her young friend. "We've all been there, and sometimes it's best just to be the bigger person and make the first move."

Annie gave her an adolescent eye roll and said, "That's what Chris told me."

Jamie laughed. "This will pass, I'm sure, and you will be fine until the next drama rolls along."

With another eye roll, Annie turned and went on up the stairs.

Jamie went to use the bathroom and then she wandered into the kitchen, and found Chris and Mary in the middle of a discussion which they discontinued when she came in.

"I'm sorry," she said. "I didn't mean to interrupt anything."

Mary smiled. "It's fine. We were just talking about Annie. She is going through some growing pains with her friends."

"I know," Jamie answered. "I just heard all about it. I backed up what you both told her by telling her that sometimes you have to be the bigger person and make the first move."

Mary smiled at Jamie. "Thank you. You know that she thinks the world of you."

"I'm kind of fond of her myself," she answered. Then she noticed Chris looking at her intently. She wasn't sure what to say next, but there was a sudden noise from the other room, indicating that it was time for the 2nd half kickoff. Chris grinned at her and then winked before he left for the other room.

Mary sighed. "Everybody talks about how difficult going through childbirth is. It turns out that is the easy part."

Jamie understood her statement more than Mary knew, but she couldn't let her know that, so she just smiled and said, "I just hope that someday I am fortunate enough to find out."

"I hope so too," Mary told her. "By the way did I hear you say that your family is in Florida?"

"My mother is," Jamie answered. "My father died last winter."

"I am so sorry about that," Mary replied. "Is your mother planning to return here for the holidays. Or are you going there?"

Jamie sighed. "My mother hasn't said anything about that to me. I'm not going down there for Thanksgiving. It's too short of a break from school and the flights are probably expensive because of the holiday. As far as Christmas goes, I haven't really given it much thought."

"Well, you are welcome to join us for Thanksgiving if you would like," Mary told her. "I'm kind of a traditionalist where the holidays are concerned. I go all out. However, if you are considering flying to Florida for Christmas, you better get a jump on making plane reservations. They book up quickly."

"I know," Jamie told her. "I guess that I need to talk to my mother to see what her thoughts are."

At that point, there was a large cheer from the other room. "I guess we better get back in there."

"I think so," Jamie agreed.

The rest of the game was pretty exciting, and the Buckeyes were able to pull off a win. Most of the group remained for one more round of food, but eventually the guests began to gather up their football paraphernalia and their dirty dishes and say their good-byes. Jamie offered Mary her help in cleaning up. She only grinned, sat down in a recliner and looked at her son.

"I don't need any help, but Chris might."

Chris looked at Jamie and spoke. "It's an arrangement that we have. She does certain things for me and in exchange, I do things for her. Cleaning up after parties is one of my things. I am supposed to have a young helper, but I see that she has disappeared again. I don't feel like arguing with her today, so yes, I would appreciate some help."

Jamie smiled and walked over to the table and began gathering up empty dishes. Her heart was light thinking that this is how families are supposed to be. Even if things weren't perfect, they lived and worked together with a certain harmony.

Inside the kitchen, Chris was putting leftover food into plastic containers and stacking the dirty dishes. The dishwasher was open, and he looked at it and said, "Do you mind rinsing the silverware and putting it into the washer?"

"I can do that," she answered.

They worked quietly for a few minutes and then Chris spoke. "We have a couple of baby goats in the barn that were born this past week. After we finish, do you want to go out and see them?"

"I would love that," she told him. After another moment, she asked him a question. "I'm just curious. What does your mom do for you?"

He laughed. "She does my laundry. I don't mind cleaning up my apartment, but I don't want to deal with washing my clothes, especially with how grimy some of my things get when I have been out in the barn and the fields with the animals. I have to bring it to the basement and pick it up when it's done, but it's still a good deal."

Jamie laughed. "I would agree with that."

A little while later, the two of them walked outside and as soon as they entered the barn, Jamie could tell that Chris was in his element. He led her to a stall in the back. It was divided into two parts, and in each section, there was a mother and a baby goat.

Jamie stood at the gate and stared at the adorable little creatures. "Oh, my goodness. What cute little things," she said. "They are already running around."

Chris smiled. "It doesn't take long for them to walk," he told her. "We just pen them up to make sure that they are all right. We'll probably put them out with the others in a week or so unless we happen to get a cold snap."

"Can I pet them?" she asked.

"Put your hand through the rail over here," he told her. "That one came up to Annie this morning, but the other one wouldn't. Animals are like people. They have different personalities."

Jamie did as he told her and sure enough the little creature came up to her and started nuzzling her hand. This went on for several minutes until the mama goat suddenly made a noise and the baby skittered back to her and began to nurse.

"I guess time is up," she said.

"It would seem so," he answered.

Jamie attempted to get the other baby to come to her, but he wasn't having it, so the two of them started to walk back toward the door.

"I haven't stopped thinking about Annie since last night," she said. "Then after seeing that she was so upset over a little thing like a fight with her friend, I wondered if she really could handle hearing such serious news. I feel sorry for your mom. It is a difficult situation."

"It certainly is," he answered. Then he stopped at the door of the barn and looked at her.

"I dreamed about Kyle last night for the first time in a long time," he said. "I guess our visit with Granny and our making of the list must have brought it on."

Jamie stared back at him. "That's strange. I dreamed about my father last night. Granny is more powerful than we thought."

"I guess," he answered and then opened the door. The two of them walked silently back to the house.

Once she was there, Jamie began to gather up her things and prepare to go home. She thanked Mary and Jake for inviting her, and they told her that they would probably have another party in a few weeks, and she was welcome to join them. Chris walked her as far as the door and thanked her for helping him clean up. She made a joking comment about how she was glad to help in the cause of keeping him presentable. Then she waved and went to her car.

Jamie spent the next day cleaning her little house and doing laundry. During the evening she worked on plans for upcoming school projects. The only person that she talked to the whole day was her mother, because she took Mary's words to heart and decided to broach the subject of the holidays.

She started by telling her that she had been invited by friends for Thanksgiving dinner. Then she went on to say that if either of them was going to fly in December, they probably should make reservations. Following that statement there was a definite silence on the phone. Then her mother dropped a bombshell on her.

"Oh, Jamie," she began. "I didn't realize that you were even considering coming here for the holidays. I'm sorry, but I have booked a Christmas cruise with my friends. We board the ship on the 21st of December and don't return until the 28th. Then we are going to stay in Miami through New Year's. All our reservations are non-refundable. I'll be back in Sarasota on the 3rd. Maybe you could be here when I get back and we could have a couple of days together."

"I'm afraid not," Jamie answered. "I have to return to work on the 4th."

"Couldn't you take a couple of days off?" her mother asked.

"I am a new employee," Jamie explained, "and the last thing I'm going to do is ask for time off right after a two-week vacation."

"Well, that's a shame. I'll just have to mail you your gift. Maybe you can come down on your spring break."

"Mom, I'm getting another call. I'll talk to you later. Bye," Jamie said to her mother, so that she could end the conversation.

Then she hit the disconnect button on her phone. After a few minutes of feeling sorry for herself, something occurred to her. Like Mary, she was a traditionalist, and she really didn't want to spend the holidays with her mother and her partying friends on a beach. She would rather spend them here alone in the cold and hopefully with some snow. The other thing that she realized was that she had to face the fact that her mother didn't really care about spending time with her. If she was ever to have a family life, she was going to have to find a way to create one for herself.

The next couple of days at school were hectic. Leslie had sprained her ankle while in Milwaukee and she would not be back until later in the week, so Jamie was busy helping her substitute and dealing with her own class.

On Thursday morning, Jamie woke up to the sound of her phone ringing thirty minutes before her alarm was due to go off. It was the one call system from the school district. Apparently, there was a water main break near the school, and because the water supply had to be shut off, school was cancelled for the day. She smiled, thinking that as unfortunate as it was for the people who had their water shut off, this was like a gift from heaven for Jamie. She turned off her alarm and then slept for another hour.

When she woke, she fixed herself a cup of coffee and took it to the living room and sat on the couch. Her school bag was waiting patiently for her by the door. There was a momentary temptation to drag out her lesson plans once more, but that idea quickly passed. She did, however, go to the bag and retrieve her laptop.

It appeared to be a beautiful day, so she opened the windows before sitting down and opening her computer. Once she did, she just sat and stared for a moment, wondering what exactly she was going to do first. For some strange reason the thought of the list popped into her mind, so she went to the kitchen and returned with it. After staring at it for a moment, she googled the name Kyle Wilson.

One of the first items that came up was a newspaper article about his fatal accident. Jamie quickly skimmed through the story. The only new thing that she learned was that it was Chris who had found his brother lying under the tractor. This nearly brought a tear to her eye. It was devastating enough to lose a brother so unexpectedly, but to be the person to make the discovery was almost too sad to think about.

A few minutes later, Jamie was reading Kyle's obituary. What she wanted to learn was how the surviving family members were listed. Would it say that he was survived by a daughter, Annie, or a sister Annie? Interestingly, it said neither. The obituary was written in an unusual way. It stated that Kyle was survived by family members, Jake, Mary, Chris, and Annie. What Jamie concluded from that was that even at that time, Mary, and or Jake were considering raising Annie as their child. These were questions that were not her place to ask, but she was certainly curious about the truth of the situation.

While thinking about obituaries, it occurred to her that it would be interesting to read the obituaries of Brenda and Dora, but she had no idea what their last names were. She considered calling Leslie to ask her, but something told her not to do that. After a moment of thought she went to the archive section of the newspaper and began searching for articles about fatal accidents.

Twenty minutes later, she found what she was looking for. The article stated that two former Valene School District teachers were killed in a head on collision on I-18. It went on to say that both women were respected teachers and that they would be missed by the community. From there she was able to link to their obituaries. Neither of them were survived by a spouse or children. Both women still used their maiden names. Brenda's obituary did state that she was preceded in death by a former husband. Apparently, Brenda had been married and divorced and then her ex-husband had died, which was interesting. From there Jamie googled the ex-husband's name and found his obituary. The one thing that stood out from that was a request that in lieu of flowers, donations could be made to the local chapters of alcoholics anonymous and ala-non. That gave her a large clue as to why Brenda may have been divorced.

There was one other interesting thing that jumped out to her. Kyle, Brenda, and Dora were all buried in the same cemetery. Jamie was almost certain that she remembered seeing the cemetery just outside of town when she had traveled to Valene or Madison.

A cool breeze suddenly blew in from the window, and Jamie looked over at the chair to see if it moved. Although the curtains had fluttered, the chair remained still. Then she remembered her plan to research the house and the property. After she went and fixed herself another cup of coffee, she went back to work. Eventually, she found herself on the site of the county recorder's office in Valene.

After doing a search on the property, she found it all a little overwhelming, so she decided to call the office and ask for some help. The lady who answered her call was extremely helpful. She explained that all deed transfers were a matter of public record, and they received requests for records all the time. Then she offered to email the information about the property. Jamie explained that she didn't have a printer and she asked if they could print them for her if she came there. The woman said that she could do that for a small printing fee. Jamie then made an arrangement to pick up the papers later that afternoon.

A little while later, she headed out of town on her mission to retrieve the property records. Just as she left Riley, she noticed the cemetery where most of the people on *"the list"* were buried. On a whim, she stopped and pulled through the main gate. The cemetery wasn't overly large, but it wasn't small either. She didn't have time to go through every row of headstones to find the graves of any of the three people that she knew were buried in this place.

There didn't seem to be anyone around, so she just drove slowly through the main section. As she was driving, for some strange reason a blue jay flew very low right in front of her windshield. The bird continued on to her right and flew to a group of headstones at the top of a hill. Jamie was then suddenly compelled to turn into the next section and drive to the top of the hill. When she reached the end of the drive, she looked around and didn't see any familiar names, so she turned around and headed back down the hill.

When she was halfway down, she just happened to spot Dora's grave out of the corner of her eye. It was in a row which was to her right, about three or four headstones down. She pulled the car over and walked to the grave. After reading the headstone, she looked around to see if any other family members were buried near her. There were no headstones in the area with her last name on them, but surprisingly, or maybe not so surprisingly, Brenda and her ex-husband were buried right next to her. Jamie stood and stared at the graves for a few minutes. As she read the dates of their deaths, it occurred to her that the anniversary of the accident had passed recently and there were fresh flowers on the headstones. Her mind immediately went to Bessie, and she concluded that that was who was taking care of their graves.

After returning to her car, she looked around to see if her bird friend was going to give her more guidance. Then she told herself that that was ridiculous. It was just a coincidence.

As she was about to leave the cemetery, she happened to see a stone with the name Wilson on it, so she stopped again. It took a couple of minutes, but she was able to locate Kyle's grave. There were fresh flowers on his grave also. Jamie scanned his headstone and realized that his birthday was this month, and she presumed that Mary had brought the flowers. As she left the cemetery, she felt an overwhelming sense of sadness for three people who had died suddenly, and possibly before their time.

Back at her home, she opened the envelope that she had received at the recorder's office. After reading for a few minutes, she picked up her phone and called Chris. He answered on the 2nd ring.

"Hi Jamie. I was just getting ready to call you. What's up?" he asked.

"I did some research on the property, and I learned something interesting that I was going to share with you. What were you going to call me about?"

"Well," he began. "I got a call from Granny a little while ago. She wants to see the two of us again."

Chapter Seven

"Really?" Jamie asked. "Did she say why?"

Chris let out a little laugh. "No, in typical Granny fashion, she said very little," he answered. "I told her that I would talk to you and maybe we would come and see her this weekend. What did you learn about the property?"

"I did some researching online and then I ended up going to the county recorder's office this afternoon," she said. "They gave me a printout of the property records clear back to the 19th century. It seems that that the property that this house is on was once a part of a larger farm which included the property where you live."

"Huh," he said. "That is interesting. I'd like to see that, and I imagine that Dad would too."

"You're welcome to look at it," she told him. "I don't have a printer, but I can make you a copy at school tomorrow."

"I have a better idea," he answered. "Mom's making chili tonight. Why don't you come over for dinner and we can all look at it, and we can make a copy on our printer. Then we can go out and see the goats again. The other little one has now decided to be friendly."

"I would love that," she answered. "Are you sure that will be all right with your mom?"

"She always makes plenty," he said. "Besides, she adores you."

"She does? Did she say that?"

"No, but I know Mom well enough that I can tell that she really likes you," he chuckled. "I'm going to be coming by your place in about ten minutes. Would you like me to pick you up?"

"That would be great," she replied, "but please let your mother know that I am coming."

"I will," he said. "See you in a few."

A little while later, Jamie sat with the Wilson's eating Mary's chili. It was a little spicey, but delicious at the same time. Jake was examining the papers that had come from the recorder's office.

"I had an idea that our farm was part of a larger farm at one time," he said. "I always meant to do some research like this, but I've never gotten around to it. Do you mind if I make a copy of this?"

"Please do," Jamie told him. "I don't have a copier anymore. I had one in our house, but it was out of ink and my mother thought that it was broken, so she threw it out when she was packing to move." After letting out a sigh, she continued. "She was in quite the hurry to get to Florida."

Mary looked at her for a moment and then spoke. "Did you do any checking into flights in December?"

Jamie shook her head. "No, I don't need to. I called her last Sunday, and she informed me that she and her friends are going on a Christmas cruise and then spending the New Year in Miami."

It was quiet in the room for a moment. It was Annie who spoke next. "You can spend Christmas with us, Jamie. You won't have to be alone."

The words of her young friend warmed Jamie's heart. "Thank you, Annie. That's very sweet of you to offer."

At that point Chris changed the subject. "Are you ready to go and see the goats?"

Jamie smiled at him, feeling grateful that the subject had been steered away from her family situation. "Yes, let's do that now."

This time Chris opened the gate and let her enter the stall. The baby goat that had allowed her to pet it the last time came right to her, and she spent a few minutes cuddling and playing with it. Then in the other stall, it took some time, but the other baby eventually did come to her and nuzzled her hand. Chris watched her the entire time without saying anything.

When she came out of the 2nd stall, he smiled at her. "You enjoyed that, didn't you?"

"I did," she answered. "I am an animal lover."

The two of them stood there for a moment and neither made a move toward the door. Eventually, Chris spoke. "Jamie, that's too bad about your mother going away on Christmas. I just assumed that you would go down there for the holidays. My parents and I don't always see eye to eye, but I can't imagine them going off and spending the holidays without me or Annie."

Jamie thought for a moment. "You know what. When I first got off the phone with her, I was very upset. Then after I gave some thought to the situation, I realized something."

"What was that?"

"I didn't really want to spend my Christmas vacation in Florida watching my mother party with her friends. I would rather be here, relaxing during my time off, and hoping for a white Christmas," she told him.

Chris looked at her for a moment. "I get that," he said, "but it still hurts that she didn't give any thought to you at the most family-oriented time of the year, doesn't it?"

At his words, Jamie felt tears well up in her eyes, so she only nodded at him. Then suddenly, he reached out and pulled her into a warm embrace. Because it had been such a long time since she had felt so warm and safe, her tears flowed more freely.

Eventually, Jamie began to feel somewhat awkward, so she moved a little away from him. "I'm sorry for getting so upset. I don't know what came over me."

He smiled at her. "You are only human, Jamie. We all fall apart sometimes." Then he walked over to where a paper towel roll was hanging off the wall and tore off a piece, which he handed to her.

After she wiped her eyes and face off, he asked her a question. "Do you want to go see Granny tomorrow night?"

"I would love to do that," she told him.

"Great," he answered. "Would you prefer, Italian, Mexican, or Chinese for dinner this time?"

Jamie thought for a moment. "I do love lasagna," she said with a smile.

"Benito's it is," he told her. "I'll pick you up at five again and we'll see Granny and then go to dinner."

"I will look forward to that," she replied.

The next day after school, Jamie gathered her things and some papers that Leslie's sub had ready for her. Her ankle was healing, and Joe was driving her home later that night. Jamie was planning to take them to her house the next morning.

It was just about 4 o'clock when she pulled her car into the driveway. Just as she closed her car door, she heard an unexpected sound. It was a very loud moo. Looking up, she saw a cow standing in her yard. For a moment, she just stood there somewhat stunned. Then she pulled out her cell phone and called Chris. He answered almost immediately.

"Hi Jamie. What's up?"

"Hey," she began. "It's not what is up, but it's what I'm looking at. There is a cow standing in my yard."

"Are you kidding me?" he asked.

"Chris, I may be a city girl, but I know a cow when I see one."

"I will be right there," he said, and just before he disconnected the call, she heard him yell, "Dad...!"

When he pulled up five minutes later, she had dropped her bag in the house, and was back out on the front porch. Chris parked the truck in her driveway and Annie jumped out of the passenger side. Just as he got out of the truck, his phone rang. After talking for a moment, he pulled a couple of orange flairs out of the back of the truck. Then he walked out on the road and motioned her and Annie to follow him.

"Dad has found several more cows out down the road," he told them. "I'm going to shoo this one back down that way, and Dad and I will try to get them back in the lower gate. The break in the fence isn't far from there. Mom's going to guard it. I'm going to light these flairs and then the two of you stand here and warn any cars coming down the road to keep an eye out for animals on the road."

"Sure," Jamie answered.

He lit the flairs and started to walk off and then he turned back and looked at Annie. "Do me a favor and call Granny. Tell her about the cows and let her know that I won't make it tonight. I'll call her tomorrow morning."

Then he turned around and started moving toward the cow, waving his arms while yelling, "Yah, Yah!" To Jamie's surprise, the cow turned and began to move in the other direction.

Annie giggled and Jamie said, "I guess that's how it's done. Does this happen a lot?"

"Not very often, but it can happen at any time. I'm just glad that my horse wasn't out."

"Are horses harder to catch than cows?" Jamie asked.

"Mine is," Annie told her. "She likes to run, and she is stubborn. The thing about cows is that once you get one inside the gate, the others will follow."

About that time a car turned onto the road. Jamie walked over and explained the situation to the driver while Annie called her grandmother. Another car immediately followed the first and Jamie once again explained the situation.

There were no more cars for the next thirty minutes and eventually Chris called Jamie and told her that all the cows were back in the pasture. He asked her to put out the flairs. They were going to fix the fence enough to hold them in tonight, and they would make better repairs in the morning.

Then Mary called her and asked her if she and Annie would go to the house and heat up some leftover chili. She said that she would be up in a little while once Jake and Chris got started on the repairs and she didn't need to chase away any cows.

The two of them drove over to the Wilson house and went into the kitchen. Once they had gotten everything out, Annie said that she needed to go out to the barn and see to her horse. After she left, Jamie looked around and decided to make some grilled cheese sandwiches and some fried potatoes to go with the chili which was nearly gone.

Mary came in right after Annie returned from the barn. She was pleased to see that a nice dinner was waiting for all of them. Jake had taken Chris to get his truck and the two of them were only about ten minutes behind her.

For the second night in a row, Jamie ate chili with the Wilson family. It was quiet for a few minutes and then she looked over at Chris and noticed blood running down his hand.

"Do you know that you are bleeding?" she asked him.

He immediately looked at his hand. "I cut it on some barbed wire," he said. "I thought that had stopped."

He got up and went to the kitchen sink and washed and dried the wound. Then he reached into a nearby cabinet and fished out a band-aide which he placed over the cut. Without further comment, he returned to his seat and continued to eat his dinner.

"Chris," Annie asked. "I called Granny like you asked. She said that was fine, but why were you going to see her tonight?"

He did not immediately respond, and Jamie looked over at Mary who was looking at him and apparently interested in the answer to Annie's question.

"You were going to see Granny tonight?" she asked.

Chris shot a glance across the table to Annie and then answered his mother's question.

"She called me this morning and asked me to come over," he told her.

"Why?" Mary wanted to know.

Chris shrugged and said, "Who knows with Granny?"

Mary didn't respond and went back to eating her chili, but Annie wasn't satisfied. She looked back and forth from Chris to Jamie. After a moment she selected Jamie to question.

"Were you two going to see Granny without me?"

Jamie was caught between a rock and a hard place. She looked over at Chris for help. The two exchanged a long look, and then Chris spoke.

"We went to see her last week, when you were at Lacey's."

Mary now set down her spoon and asked a question. "Am I missing something here?"

"We were all three curious as to why Granny told Jamie to take care of the chair," Chris explained. "So, we decided to just ask her. The easiest time to go was when I took her groceries to her last Friday night, and like I said, Annie was at Lacey's."

"And did Granny give you an explanation as to why she said that about the chair?" Mary asked.

Chris shrugged. "Not really," he said. "She just did her thing where she closes her eyes and seems to be listening to someone. I asked her who she was talking to, but she wouldn't say. She basically told us not to worry about the chair. Then she told Jamie that she was brought here and there was a plan and not to worry about it."

"But she called you today and asked you to come back?" Jake asked.

"She did," Chris answered.

"Just you?" Mary wanted to know.

Now Chris and Jamie exchanged another look, and this time he grinned at her. "No, she asked me to bring Jamie too. I think she likes her. She asked her to call her Granny."

"So, the two of you were going tonight, without me again?" Annie said with an adolescent whine.

"Yes, we were. I thought that you and Lacey made up and you were going there tonight," he told her.

"Today is her mother's birthday, so they are going out to eat," Annie explained. "I'm going tomorrow night."

"Then, can we assume that the two of you are going to make your visit to Granny tomorrow?" Mary asked.

"I haven't had a chance to discuss that with Jamie yet," Chris answered.

"If you are going, would you mind doing the grocery run and saving me the trip?" Mary wanted to know.

Chris nodded. That would work.

Annie looked over at Jamie. "Do you want to go with him, Jamie?"

Before she could answer, Chris intervened. "Have you taken care of your horse tonight?"

Annie nodded. "I have." To Chris's relief, Annie's phone rang at that moment, and she asked to be excused.

When she was gone it was quiet for a moment and then Mary grinned at Chris. Then she looked at Jamie. "I really appreciate you going above and beyond with dinner. This was way better than just reheated chili."

"It was really no big deal," she told her. "I enjoyed doing it. It has been a long day though. I should be heading home. Can I help you clean up?"

"No, I will take care of it," she said. "Do you want to help me, honey?"

"I would be glad to," Jake answered, and the two of them began to carry dishes to the kitchen.

Chris motioned Jamie to follow him to the front room. They stood at the front door quietly for a moment until Chris spoke.

"I guess we've been outed," he said.

"I think so," she agreed. "In a way, I'm glad. I like your parents and I felt funny keeping secrets from them."

"To be honest, I am kind of relieved myself," he said, "and we didn't give them all the details, so I think they kind of blew it off to Granny's idiosyncrasies."

"That was the impression that I got too," she answered.

"Are we on for tomorrow?" he asked.

Jamie smiled at him. "Sure."

"All right. I'll call you when we finish with the fence," he told her.

"That will work," she said. Then there was an awkward moment, and Jamie had the feeling that he was considering kissing her. However, she didn't have time to analyze her feelings about that because there was suddenly the sound of Annie's footsteps coming down the stairs.

Jamie then just smiled and said, "I'll see you tomorrow."

"Good-night, Jamie," he said as she made her way to her car.

The next morning, Jamie headed over to Leslie's house to take her class's papers to her. Her boyfriend Joe was there tending to her every need. Jamie liked him right away. He was pleasant and jovial and seemed to have a personality that matched Leslie's. Jamie didn't stay long because Leslie said that she had an appointment in Valene with her uncle who was an orthopedic nurse practitioner. She was actually glad to get away because she was looking forward to getting the call from Chris.

On the way home, she thought about how she felt about the situation with Chris. He was the first man that she had actually been interested in since her breakup with Craig. She knew that she was still vulnerable, but there was something about Chris that she couldn't seem to resist. The warning bells were getting fainter and fainter.

It was around 11:00 when he did call, and he told her that he was going to take a quick shower and then he would be right over. After he picked her up, they went straight to Granny's apartment and took her to her hairdresser. Then they went to the drugstore and picked up an extensive list of items. Some of which were for Granny, and some were for Mary. Chris seemed to find this chore a little overwhelming, so Jamie stepped in and picked out the items and sorted them in the cart for separate billing. When that was accomplished, they headed to the grocery store to pick up the order. It wasn't time for Granny to be finished, so they went to her apartment and put the groceries away.

A little while later, they had Granny all settled back into her apartment. She seemed a little tired, but happy to have visitors. They chatted about small things for a while. Then Chris eventually got to the point, and asked Granny if there was a particular reason that she wanted him and Jamie to come back.

Granny smiled. "I just enjoyed your company so much the last time you were here," she said, "and you two are so adorable together."

Jamie knew her face reddened and she wasn't sure exactly how to respond to that comment. Chris attempted to answer her, but whatever he was going to say sort of fell flat.

"Granny…"

"What dear?" she asked.

He paused and then said, "That was a nice thing to say."

Granny then turned to Jamie and stared at her for a moment, and she got the strange feeling that she was *listening* again.

"You missed one the other day," she said.

Jamie was confused. "I'm sorry. I don't understand. What did I miss?"

"At the cemetery," she told her. "You didn't find everybody on your list."

The shock on Jamie's face had to be apparent. She hoped that her mouth did not actually drop open. "How did you know that I was at the cemetery? I didn't tell anyone about that. Not even Chris."

Granny only smiled and said, "It doesn't matter how I know. Just check your list and look again. Now I am a little tired and I think that I would like to take a nap before my girl comes in with dinner. So, would the two of you excuse me so that I can do that?"

Jamie looked over at Chris who was completely confused at this point. She made a motion to him that they should just leave, so they both told Granny good night. Outside in the truck, Chris didn't start it, but he looked at her and said, "Did you go to the cemetery?"

She then explained to him about how she had researched the obituaries of the people on their list and realized that they were all buried in the same cemetery. Then she told him about passing the cemetery on the way to the recorder's office and how she stopped on a whim. She also told him about the blue jay and how it led her to Brenda and Dora's graves and how she was able to find Kyle's grave.

"Who did you miss then?" he asked.

Jamie thought for a moment and then it came to her. "Carol's mother, Liz." Then she picked up her phone and googled the woman's obituary. It didn't take long for her to find out that she was also buried in the same cemetery.

Chris looked at his watch. "It's a little early for dinner," he said.

"What do you want to do?" she asked.

He grinned at her. "We are going to the cemetery."

A few minutes later, the two of them were standing at Dora and Brenda's graves. There was little to say at that point, so they returned to the truck and drove over to Kyle's grave. When they got out of the truck the second time, it had suddenly become overcast, and Jamie noticed a definite drop in the temperature. She followed Chris as he walked over to the grave of his brother. He stood quietly for a moment and then he spoke softly.

"It was so wrong. It should never have happened." Jamie wasn't sure what to do, but she did reach out and touch his arm. He responded by raising his arm up and putting it around her.

"Kyle and I were going to run the farm together," he said in a hoarse voice. "We had such big plans."

He then squeezed her shoulder a little harder, and Jamie suspected that he didn't even realize that he was doing that.

"Is that why you drive yourself so hard on the farm and try to make it better?" she asked.

Chris looked down at her and nodded. "I want to make him proud."

Jamie smiled and said, "I'm sure that he is."

Then suddenly Chris seemed to break out of the spell of sadness that had been hanging over him. "Let's see if we can find Liz," he said.

Not knowing what else to do, they circled the cemetery twice looking for headstones that had the name Patterson on them. They were just about to give up when Jamie suddenly spotted one. A few minutes later, they were standing over the grave that they had been looking for.

There were a couple of interesting things that they learned. One was that apparently, Carol's father was still alive, because his name was on the headstone, but there was no death date. The other thing was that there was a grave right next to her of a young man by the name of Roger Patterson, who apparently died at the age of 32.

Jamie looked at her phone and the browser was still open to Liz's obituary. She scanned it and sure enough, she was preceded in death by a son, Roger. After showing it to Chris, she said, "I'm pretty sure that one of Carol's twins is named Roger. That makes sense."

A cool breeze suddenly blew through the cemetery and Jamie shivered a little. "Let's get out of here," Chris said.

The lasagna at Geppetto's was delicious. Over dinner the two of them talked about a variety of topics while avoiding the subject of people who had died. When they finished, they decided to order tiramisu and take it to Jamie's house and eat it.

When they got out of the truck, in her driveway, both of them noticed that the temperature had dropped sharply in the last hour. While they were eating their dessert, Jamie asked him about winter in Wisconsin. He told her that it could be quite cold and snowy. There was another piece of information that he shared with her; the electric grid in their area was not very reliable, and it wasn't unusual for the power to be out for several days at a time during a snowstorm.

This was a cause for concern for Jamie because the fireplace didn't work, and she was not comfortable with those portable gas heaters. "Does your fireplace keep your house heated?" she asked.

"No," he told her. "We have a good-sized generator, so we have power and heat all over the house. Unfortunately, it is not connected to the garage or my apartment, so I have to move back into the house during power outages." Apparently, he read her mind because he smiled at her. "I'm sure that Mom will insist that you come and stay with us. We have plenty of room. We usually have a game night or something when there is a snowstorm."

Jamie returned his smile and said, "That sounds like fun."

At that point, Chris looked at his watch. "It is getting kind of late."

"This has been an interesting day," she told him. "The drugstore, the grocery, visiting Granny, searching through the cemetery, and dinner."

He laughed. "We have been kind of busy, haven't we?" Then after another moment, he asked her a question.

"Do you have a theory about who Granny is talking to?"

Jamie thought for a moment. "Not really. Sometimes I think that I do, but then the next day

I change my mind completely. What about you? Do you ever have a sense that Kyle is around?"

"There are times that I think that I do, but then I wonder if it is my imagination or just my desire to have him near," he said.

"I know," she told him. "It is the same way with my father."

After a moment of silence, Chris stood up and Jamie did the same. The two of them walked to the front door. There was another moment of awkwardness, and then Jamie happened to notice the place on his hand where he had cut himself the night before. Without even thinking about it, she reached out and took his hand.

"That looks kind of nasty," she said. "It's not infected, is it?"

Chris grinned. "Not a chance. Mom has been chasing me around with antibiotic cream."

After another quiet moment, Chris pulled his hand away from her and reached up and stroked her cheek. Then suddenly, they were kissing, and Jamie felt herself being pulled away in a wave of passion that she had never experienced before. When he eventually pulled away from her, she knew that this man could totally own her if he wanted to, and she didn't even care.

"Jamie, I…uh…you are the first girl that I have let in since…in a long time. It feels good. You make me happy. I just need to know if you are ready and open to this. It's kind of…"

"Scary?" she said. "I understand what you are saying. It is kind of scary, but I think that we have already passed the point of deciding if we want to let down our walls…at least I have."

Chris's only response was to kiss her again. This time when he pulled away, he smiled and said, "I'm going to go home now. I don't think that we should push this too far too soon. I feel like we are looking at the possibility of something great, and we should take it slowly."

This time she was the one to stroke his cheek. "I think you are right."

He gave her one more quick kiss and said, "Good night. I'll call you tomorrow."

"Good night," she answered.

After he was in his truck, and backing out of the driveway, Jamie closed and locked the door.

When she turned around, she stopped and stared. Did she just see the chair move ever so slightly?"

She shook her head and spoke into the air. "I don't know who you are, but ...thank you."

Chapter Eight

On Monday morning, Jamie picked up Leslie on the way to school. She was determined not to miss another day due to *"her stupid ankle"*. Even though she probably still should have been using crutches, she insisted on limping to her room. Jamie, Kim, and Gina helped get her set up in her room and devised a schedule to cover her extra duties. The principal assigned aides to stay in her room as much as possible.

At the end of the day, Jamie was very tired, and she wondered if it would have been easier if Leslie had taken more time off. As soon as she got home, she changed into sweats and a T-shirt and then she decided that a frozen pizza was in order for dinner.

Just after she closed the oven door, her phone began to ring. She smiled because she hoped that it was Chris. It wasn't him, but Annie. This was a little surprising at this time of day.

"Hi Annie. What's up?"

"Are you busy?" she wanted to know. "I was hoping I could come over."

"Sure," she answered. "I just put in a frozen pizza. I'll never eat it all. Do you want some?"

"Sounds great," she answered. "Barney and I will be right there."

Twenty minutes later, while the two of them were sitting at her table munching on pepperoni pizza, Jamie decided to just ask Annie what was on her mind.

"I kind of need a favor," she answered.

"And what would that be?"

"Last year, Lacey and I convinced Chris to take us to this really cool Haunted House in Valene. He was nice enough to drive us there and he even paid for the tickets, which weren't cheap."

"That's nice," Jamie answered. "So, I'm gathering that you are wanting him to take you again?"

"Well, yes, but there is a problem. You see after we bought the tickets last year, we got as far as the door and chickened out. We ran back to the car without ever going in. The tickets were non-refundable, and he was kind of pissed."

"I see," Jamie said thoughtfully. "So, are you now hitting me up to take you?"

"Oh, no." she replied. "I want you to convince Chris to take us again. Lacey's parents are going out of town this weekend, so she is staying with me. We have the money to pay for our own tickets. Mom doesn't like the idea of haunted houses, so we came up with a plan."

"Which is?"

"We want you to tell Chris that you want to go to this haunted house," she said. "You know he will take you. Then we will just sort of hitch a ride along with the two of you."

"Hmm," Jamie answered. "That is an interesting plan, but somewhat elaborate. Did it occur to you to just ask him? From what I've seen, he's pretty good to you most of the time."

Annie didn't respond but looked at her with an adolescent stare.

Jamie tried not to smile and reached over to pick up her phone. Chris answered her call after the third ring.

"Hey," he said. "I was just thinking about calling you. What's up?"

"I have a little situation here. Is there any possibility you could come over here for a few minutes?" she asked.

"Is there something wrong?" he wanted to know.

"No, nothing like that," she told him. "It will just be easier to explain in person."

"All right," he answered. "I'll be right over."

He arrived about fifteen minutes later, and he was soon sitting at the table eating the last of the pizza. After he heard the story of Annie and Lacey's plan, he looked at the young girl and said, "Are you kidding me? Why didn't you just ask me?"

Annie shrugged and said, "I don't know."

Chris stared at her for a moment and then he looked at Jamie and laughed. "You just got played."

"What do you mean?"

"This isn't about her being afraid to ask me for something," he said. "Never in her life has she been afraid of that. Her requests to me are endless. I think what we have going on here is a little matchmaking. Am I right, sis?"

Annie's face turned red and then she suddenly jumped up and said, "I forgot to do my barn chores. I better get home before Dad notices. Come on Barney." Then within thirty seconds the two of them were out the door.

Chris burst out laughing, but Jamie was somewhat confused. "What just happened here?"

"Don't you see? Annie has decided that we are a match," he explained. "So, she was trying to set us up on a date to the haunted house."

"Ahh," Jamie answered suddenly seeing what he was trying to tell her. Then after a moment, she grinned at him and then she asked him a question.

"Do you think that we are a match?"

He gave her a long look and then said, "Come over here and we'll see if we can figure this out."

Jamie stood up and went over and sat on his lap. "Would you like to go to a haunted house with me next weekend?" he asked her.

"I'll go, but I expect you to stay close to my side every minute," she said.

"Not a problem," he told her just before he began to kiss her.

They sat quietly kissing for a few minutes. Eventually they pulled apart and Jamie looked past him into the living room.

"Chris?"

"What?"

"Speaking of haunted houses," she said, "the chair is moving again."

Chris turned and looked past her. "Do you think that Barney bumped it on their way out?"

Jamie shook her head. "They've been gone too long."

"Does this happen often?" he asked with a frown.

She thought for a moment. "It only seems to happen when you are around."

"Really? That is interesting. Maybe it likes me being here."

She smiled at him. "Then, let it rock."

The next day on the way to school, Leslie looked at her slyly and said, "I get the feeling something is going on with you. Do you want to give it up or are you going to make me wonder a while longer? That's fine, but you know that whatever it is, you know I will get it out of you sooner or later."

Jamie smiled at her and then told her about all the things that had been going on with Granny and her graveyard adventures.

"Hmm," she replied. "That is interesting." After a slight pause, she continued. "It sounds like you and Chris have been spending a lot of time together."

Jamie suppressed another smile as she turned into the school parking lot. "I guess you could say that we have become good friends."

Leslie let out a small laugh. "There is nothing wrong with having a *"good friend"*.

Choosing to ignore her remark, Jamie reached into the back seat and pulled out her bag. Then she looked at her friend and said, "It looks like rain, so we had better head inside."

By the end of the week, the rain had cleared out, but the temperature had dropped, creating a crisp cool weekend. Chris, Jamie, Annie, and Lacey headed to the Haunted House just after dark. "The Clown Factory", as it was called, was located in an old pipe factory which had fallen into a state of disrepair. As they waited outside, the girls were further back in line as they had met up with some of their friends from school. Jamie admitted to Chris that this was the first time in her life that she had ever been to a haunted anything.

He let out a laugh and said, "That is not true. You live in a haunted house."

Jamie thought for a moment. "I don't think my whole house is haunted. I just have a haunted rocking chair."

"I'll give you that," he agreed. "Do you think that this place will scare you though?"

"It might," she told him, "because this is manufactured horror, which is designed to frighten the very core of your being."

"I would have to agree with you," he answered.

"You know, I was just thinking," she said. "Clowns used to be loveable jolly characters who entertained children at circuses and birthday parties, but somehow they have become evil creatures who are scary and almost demonic."

"I think it is because a person who is in complete clown costume can totally conceal their identity," he explained, "which works well for the creative minds who write modern horror stories."

Jamie thought for a moment. "That makes sense," she answered.

Ten minutes later, the two of them were admitted into the first room of the building, along with a group of four who were behind them in line. The room was absolutely pitch dark. After thirty seconds of silence, there was a brief flash of light and they saw a creepy clown standing in front of them. The clown then opened the door and admitted them into another room. There were then several flashes of light, and they could tell that there were at least four clowns in the room. After a couple of rounds of light flashes, there was a thunder-like sound from above and the clowns then began to chase them down a narrow hallway where they entered another small room.

The now familiar sequence of light flashes began, but this time something different happened. During one of the longer periods of darkness, she was standing close to Chris, and they were holding hands. Suddenly she felt herself being shoved away from him and he let go of her hand. When the next flash of light came on, she realized what had happened. A clown had wrapped itself around Chris and was giving him a giant bear hug. He had let go of her hand to push it off him. The rest of the group found it somewhat amusing, but Jamie had the feeling that even though he did laugh along with everyone else, he did not find it funny.

They then maneuvered their way through the rest of the factory, waiting for flashes of light to see where the clowns would appear next in order to elicit as many screams as possible from their audience. Once they exited the back side of the factory, they followed the walkway around to the front to wait for Annie and her friends.

About fifteen minutes later, they came out laughing and talking loudly. They did manage to go all the way through this time and apparently a good time had been had by all. Annie and Lacey then asked if they could take them to a local pizza place to meet up with their friends. This was not a problem, and just a little while later, Chris and Jamie were in a booth in the corner of the restaurant, and Annie and Lacey were at a large table on the other side of the room with several of their middle-school friends.

Once their order had been taken, Jamie smiled and spoke. "I got the impression that you didn't appreciate your clown hug."

Chris shrugged and said, "I don't like being grabbed without warning. I think maybe that clown may have crossed the line a little." Then he looked at her. "Did she shove you?"

"Yes," she answered. "Not very hard though. By the way, I'll remember that thing about you not liking to be grabbed without warning."

He smiled at her. "*You* are an exception. You may grab me at any time you wish."

Jamie grinned and was about to respond when they were approached by a man and a woman that she had never met."

Chris looked up and spoke. "Hey buddy, what's going on?"

"We just got out of a movie, and we dropped in for some pizza," the man said.

"Great," Chris answered. Then he looked at Jamie and began introductions. "Jamie, this is a friend of mine from school, Eddie Vance and his girlfriend Elaine...I'm sorry I don't remember your last name."

"It's Brown," she replied with an almost stonelike face. Jamie got the impression that she was possibly insulted that Chris had forgotten her last name.

"Sorry," Chris replied, trying to recover from his faux pas. "I'm not good with names. "This is Jamie Barnes. She teaches second grade at Riley along with Leslie Mitchell."

"Oh yes," Eddie said. "How is Leslie? Is she still a little red-headed ball of fire?"

Jamie laughed. "That would be a perfect description of her. She is doing great. I enjoy working with her."

"Why don't you join us?" Chris asked. "We are doing chaperoning duty tonight because Annie is sitting over there with her friends, so we will probably be here awhile."

Eddie looked at Elaine, who shrugged as if to say, "Whatever."

Chris slid over to the other side of the booth with Jamie and Eddie and his girlfriend sat down across from them. It didn't take long then for Elaine to pull her phone out of her purse and then lose herself in it. Jamie got the impression that Eddie was a little embarrassed, but he tried to cover it up by asking Jamie typical questions about herself. A few minutes later, the conversation turned to the Clown Factory.

"Oh man," Eddie said. "I've been wanting to check that out, but…"

At this point, Elaine looked up from her phone and rolled her eyes. "Places like that are for kids, not grown adults; what a waste of money." Then she immediately returned to her phone."

Chris tried to help his friend cover his embarrassment by telling the story of the clown who got a little friendly with him. Eddie laughed, but Elaine once again looked up and the two of them exchanged a look. It almost appeared as if she were trying to tell him something. Then the moment passed, and Eddie changed the subject to another old school friend of theirs who had recently returned to Wisconsin.

During the rest of their dinner, Elaine continued to be buried in her phone, while the other three carried on a general conversation about their families and things going on in the community. Elaine declined to eat anything declaring herself, "not hungry". After Eddie barely had time to eat a second piece of pizza, Elaine announced that they really needed to leave. Then two minutes later, Jamie reached for another piece of pizza and spoke.

"Eddie seems to be a nice guy," she said.

"He's a great guy," Chris answered. "The strange thing is that our roles seemed to have reversed."

"How is that?" Jamie wanted to know, although she really did have an idea where he was going with this.

"A while back, Eddie sat back and watched me go down a road that led to disaster," he began.

"And now you are watching him go down a similar road?"

"That would be correct," he said.

"Did he try to warn you?" Jamie asked.

"He certainly did," he replied.

"Have you tried to do the same for him?"

"I have dropped a few hints," he answered. "This is not an easy territory."

"Believe me, I know," she told him. "I got the feeling though that he was a little embarrassed by her tonight."

"Yeah, I picked up on that too," he said.

At that point, Annie and Lacey walked over and sat down across from them. "We're ready to go. Who was that woman with Eddie? He stopped to say hi to me and she was kind of..."

"Rude?" Chris asked.

"Yeah," Annie replied.

"That is Elaine, his girlfriend. I am not a fan."

"Me either," Annie said with her now practically trademark eyeroll.

Chris and Jamie looked at each other and laughed.

On Wednesday evening of the following week, Jamie was sitting in the living room of her house, grading math tests. Indian summer had arrived, and she had opened her living room windows and was enjoying the fresh breeze flowing into the house. As she heard the sound of a vehicle coming down the road, she looked up, because she was hoping that it might be Chris. She hadn't seen him in a couple of days, and she thought that he might stop by because when he called the night before he had mentioned something about Chinese food sometime this week.

Somewhere deep inside of her, the now almost non-existent warning voice said, *"Girl, you are falling hard. Be careful."*

The louder and more prevalent voice spoke in the front of her mind. *"He makes you happy and there is nothing wrong with that."*

It was not Chris driving by, but a blonde woman driving slowly in a blue Toyota. Jamie shrugged and went back to her papers. A couple of minutes later, the same car passed by again, and the driver looked directly at her house. At first, she found that strange, but then she considered the possibility that the woman was lost. Then she had a chuckle with herself thinking about the woman being blonde.

When the car passed for a third time, Jamie began to feel a little uneasy, so she put her papers down and walked to the window. The last time that the car had passed, it had been heading away from the main road toward the turnoff to the Wilson's. She waited just a minute and was about to return to the couch when she spotted the driver of the car walking down the road in her direction.

The woman was not very tall, but she appeared to be at least fifty pounds overweight. When she reached Jamie's driveway, she turned and began walking toward the house. Feeling somewhat uncomfortable, with every Facebook horror warning story ringing in her ears, she picked up her phone off the table and brought up Chris's number. She didn't make the call, but she decided to have it ready just in case.

When the woman reached the door, she was breathing heavily from her walk from wherever she had left her car. Her blonde hair was obviously a home out of the box job and her clothes looked well worn.

With her phone in hand, Jamie opened the door slightly, and spoke.

"Can I help you?" she asked.

"Hello," the woman responded. "I had a flat tire down the road, and I would call AAA, but there is something wrong with my phone. I can't get the call to go through."

Jamie thought for a moment and decided that it would not be wise to hand this woman her phone and cut off all her forms of communication to the outside world.

"I've seen you driving up and down the road a few times," she said to the woman. "Are you looking for a particular place?"

The woman was quiet for a moment and then responded. "No, I came by here this morning, and I had some important papers in my car. One of them blew out and I need to find it." There was another moment of silence and then she continued. "You see, I am an officer of the court. I serve papers and if I don't find the one that I lost, I could get fired."

It was obvious that she was making up her story as she went along, and Jamie was now very uncomfortable. She was about to tell this crazy lady that she would call her a tow truck and then shut the door in her face before calling the sheriff's department to report this incident.

Then just as she opened her mouth to speak, Chris happened to drive by in his truck.

Right after he passed her driveway, he hit the brakes and began to back up. He pulled in the driveway and jumped out. Jamie was almost certain that she heard the woman say, "damn" under her breath.

Chris marched right up to the woman and asked, "What the hell are you doing here?"

The woman sighed and said, "Don't go off on one of your tangents, Chris. I had a flat tire down the road, and this was the closest house, so I walked here to ask for help."

"Well, first of all, I know damn well that you know how to change a tire. I've heard you brag about it many times," he began. "Then if you didn't want to do it yourself, we both know that there is a AAA card in your wallet."

"My phone died," she said in a voice that was almost a whine. Jamie had absolutely no idea what was going on, but she could tell by the look on Chris's face that he was angrier than she had ever seen him.

Then at that moment, to further complicate the already confused situation, Barney came bounding out of the woods and across the road. He did not stop until he reached the group that was standing at Jamie's door. The dog then simply sat down and appeared to be waiting to see what would happen next.

"I'll tell you what," Chris said to the woman. "I'll walk over to your car and if you have a flat tire, I'll change it myself, just to send you on your way."

Then he turned and began walking rapidly down the driveway. The woman followed behind him, huffing and puffing all the way.

Jamie was still standing in her doorway, stupefied, trying to figure out what had just happened. Then she noticed Annie, who had followed Barney, crossing the road. As she walked across, she stared at Chris and the woman.

When she reached Jamie, she was almost laughing. "What the devil is Cassie doing here?" she wanted to know.

Now Jamie's mouth fell open. "That woman is Cassie?" Jamie asked as she pointed in the direction that they had gone. "She is..."

"Fat as a cow?"

Jamie let out a giggle. "I was going to say...a little overweight...but your description works too."

Annie joined in with her. "Just in case you are wondering, she didn't look like that when Chris dated her. She was quite a looker when they were together."

Before Jamie could respond, the blue Toyota came flying past the house spewing a whir of stone from the side of the road. A moment later, Chris came walking back to the house. Jamie could tell by the look on his face that he was extremely angry.

Annie spoke to her in a quiet voice. "I think you are about to see a side of Chris that you have never seen before." At that moment, Jamie tended to agree.

Just as he reached the two of them, his cell phone rang and announced that his father was calling. Then she heard him utter a vial curse word that she had heard before, but never out of his mouth. He pulled his phone out of its holder and answered the call.

"Yeah"

"Shit. I'll be right there."

"What's wrong?" Annie asked.

"There is a cow having trouble giving birth right outside the barn," he said. "I've got to go." Then he looked at Jamie. "I'll be back in a little while."

After he was gone, Jamie looked at her young friend and spoke. "I am completely confused,"

"Let's go in and I will explain it to you," she giggled.

Inside the house, the two of them sat down and Annie began her story.

"Did Chris tell you that after they initially broke up that a few months later, she came back crying and begging him to take her back?" Jamie nodded.

"Well, he told her to get lost," she said, "and apparently she went into some sort of deep depression and started eating everything in her path."

"Hence the fifty or so pounds that she is overweight?"

"Yep," Annie answered. "Then to cover for her princess, her mother went all over town telling everyone who would listen, that her daughter's mental and physical state were all Chris's fault."

Jamie's eyes opened wide. "That explains his anger."

Annie nodded. "Have you ever seen a picture of her when she was still in shape?"

Jamie shook her head. "Didn't you ever look on Facebook?" Annie asked.

She shrugged. "I didn't know her last name and Chris isn't on Facebook, so I couldn't look that way."

Annie grinned and picked up her cell and began searching. After a moment, she handed her phone to Jamie, who wasn't sure if she wanted to see the picture or not.

The photo was of Cassie at the beach somewhere. She was wearing an extremely skimpy bikini and striking a pose. There was not an ounce of fat anywhere on her body. A minute later, she began rolling through some more pictures. Most of them were selfies of her, or of posed pictures that someone, possibly Chris, took of her. Jamie then went back to her timeline. After scrolling down, she realized that the last time that she had actually posted anything herself was quite some time ago.

Jamie looked up at Annie. "Wow. That is hard to imagine that the woman who was here today and this woman are the same."

"Did you notice that all the pictures are of her? She is totally all about her and her looks. Now that she lost that, she doesn't know what to do with herself."

Jamie nodded. "It's actually kind of sad,"

Annie was then quiet for a moment. "You don't have to worry about her you know. Even if she drops the weight off and becomes a looker again, it won't matter. He is over her. He is one hundred percent in love with you."

Her heart fluttered at Annie's words. "Did Chris tell you that?" she wanted to know.

"No, of course not," she said, "but he didn't have to. It's obvious, and..."

"And what?"

"I overheard Mom and Dad talking about it. It's pretty clear to them too."

"I see," Jamie answered, as she attempted to internalize this new information.

Then Annie realized that she might have been a little premature with her announcement. "Oh, I gather Chris hasn't dropped the L bomb yet. Please don't tell him what I said."

Jamie smiled. "Your secret is safe with me."

The two of them talked a little while longer and then just before dark, Annie took Barney and headed home. Jamie switched on the lamp and continued grading her math tests.

Thirty minutes later, she finished with her papers, and she realized that her stomach was beginning to growl. She looked at her phone and saw it was almost eight o'clock. Just as she was deciding to heat up a Lean Cuisine frozen meal, there was a flash of light in the driveway. That warm feeling came over her again. Chris was here.

Chapter Nine

Jamie jumped up and greeted him with a hug. The two of them stood quietly holding each other for a moment and she looked up at him and said, "Rough day?"

Chris just shook his head and said, "I've had better."

"Do you want to talk about it?" she asked.

"Not really," he answered, "but I guess you have questions."

Jamie shook her head. "Annie told me all I need to know for now. Have you had dinner?"

"No," he told her. "When I came by the first time, I was heading home to grab a quick shower. Then I was coming over here to see if you wanted to go get some Chinese. I had a couple of things that I wanted to talk to you about. Have you eaten?"

"I have not," she said. "I've been wrapped up in grading papers until just now."

Chris looked at his watch. "I don't know how long they are open."

"Why don't we just call an order in and then go pick it up and bring it back here?" she suggested.

"Excellent idea," he replied.

Less than an hour later, they were sitting at her table with various containers of Chinese food spread around. They had out paper plates and were each taking portions out of all the containers.

"So, what were you wanting to talk to me about?" she asked.

"Well," he began. "I talked to Eddie today. We actually had lunch together."

"Hmmm," she said. "Did the subject of Elaine come up?"

"For sure," he told her. "She was actually the main topic of our conversation."

"That doesn't sound good."

"It wasn't," he answered. "After they left the restaurant the other night, he confronted her about her rude behavior. They got into a big thing, and I guess he broke it off with her."

"Do you think it will stick?" she asked.

"I hope so," he answered, "but then he confessed something to me that I wasn't aware of."

"What's that?"

"Apparently, Elaine is a friend of Cassie's."

Jamie had just scooped a fork full of rice and she now stopped it halfway between her plate and her mouth. "Oh, my goodness." Then all of a sudden, several things became clear. "That's why she was prowling around here this afternoon. She was checking me out. Elaine was probably texting her the whole time we were eating pizza."

Chris nodded. "Eddie thinks that she may have snapped a couple of pictures of you too."

Jamie shuddered. "That gives me the willies."

"There was one more thing," he told her.

"What?" she was almost afraid to ask.

"Apparently, she works during the day at her father's insurance company, but she has another part time job also."

"Doing what?"

Chris grinned. "In the evenings, she has been working at The Clown Factory."

"As a clown?" she asked and then the implication of what that meant dawned on her. "That was her who shoved me away from you and hugged you."

"Yep," he answered. "I thought that it was someone I knew, but I had no idea it was Cassie."

"That is so messed up," she said.

"It sure is," he answered.

Jamie took a bite of her eggroll and asked him a question. "You said that you had a couple of things to talk to me about. What else is on your mind?"

Chris finished the last of the food on his plate, wiped his mouth and looked over at her. "Well, I wanted to tell you that Mom and Dad are going back to the lake this weekend."

"Ah," Jamie replied. "You are on Annie duty again this weekend?"

"No, I thought I was, but just before I came over here, she successfully completed her campaign to have them take her and Lacey with them," he told her.

She grinned. "She certainly has everything under control."

"That is for damn sure," he answered. "Anyway, I was wondering if you would like to spend the weekend with me?"

Jamie laid her fork down on her plate and looked up at him, fully understanding the implications of what he was asking her. Their eyes locked for a moment and she waited for the warning bells to go off somewhere inside of her, but they didn't. This man now owned her and her heart completely.

"If you aren't ready, I understand," he began.

"I'm ready," she said, with a warm smile. "I'm completely ready."

Chris returned the smile. "I am too," he told her. "I think it's time."

"Oh, I almost forgot," she replied. "Leslie said that Joe is coming into town this weekend. She wanted to know if we would like to have dinner with them Friday night."

"I think that we can manage that," he said. "Friday would be good, because we will need to take care of Granny on Saturday. I was kind of hoping we could do something special for her."

Jamie thought for a moment. "Maybe we could make a home-cooked meal for her in her apartment."

"I think she would like that," he answered. Then he yawned and looked at his watch. "I'm going to head home now. It's been a long day and the vet is going to be at the barn at 6:45 in the morning."

"I understand," she answered. "I have to be at school early for a meeting myself. By the way, what happened with the cow in labor?"

He let out a chuckle. "By the time that I got there, it had been born and was nursing."

"Is that what the vet is coming for?" she asked.

"No, we have another one shut up in the barn that is way overdue," he told her. "She has lost her last two, so we aren't hopeful. He may have to do a   c-section."

"Ohhh," she replied. "That doesn't sound good."

"Nope," he answered. "I'll help you clean up."

"Don't worry about it," she answered. "It's no big deal. I'll get it. It won't take me long, but thanks for offering."

He smiled at her and then he stood and walked toward the front door, and Jamie followed him.

Without another word, he pulled her into his arms, and they shared a long and passionate kiss. After they finished, he kept his arms around her and spoke softly.

"I'm really looking forward to this weekend," he said.

"So am I," she told him in a voice that was almost a whisper.

"I'll call you tomorrow," he answered. "Good night."

"Good night, Chris." She watched him walk to his truck, get in, and drive off. Then she returned to the kitchen, feeling happier than she had in a long time.

The dinner with Leslie and Joe was a lot of fun. They went to the same restaurant that Chris had taken Jamie to the first time the two of them had gone to dinner alone. Eddie was excited about the fact that he had had a job interview earlier that day with a company located in Madison. The position would require him to be in the city 2- 3 days a week and work at home the rest of the time. The two of them were excited because this could provide him with an opportunity to move to Valene and they could begin to make definite plans for their future.

The conversation then moved to high school memories and the four of them laughed at the high school stories that Chris and Leslie told on each other.

At one point, the subject of Eddie came up and Leslie asked about him. It got quiet at the table and Chris and Jamie exchanged a look. Then Chris told the story of their recent encounter with his girlfriend, and then the breakup that followed. He then explained about her connection to Cassie and her recent visit to Jamie's house.

At the finish of his story, Leslie said, "Poor Eddie. He's such a sweet guy. I hate that this happened to him, but I guess it was for the best."

"Yeah," Chris replied. "I think he sees that. He's not giving up though. He even told me to ask the two of you if there are any single teachers at the school."

Jamie and Leslie looked at each other and shook their heads. "Only Bessie," Leslie laughed.

After a moment though something occurred to Leslie. "Wait a minute, there is that one girl that is a kindergarten aide. What is her name? I can't remember."

"I don't know," Jamie said. "I rarely get to that part of the building. I have no idea who you are talking about. If you can't even remember her name, how do you know if she's single?"

Leslie shrugged. "I don't, but I have a feeling. Don't worry. I'll get the scoop from Sandy first thing Monday morning. She knows everything about everybody." Then she picked up her fork and went to work on the last of her baked potato. Jamie giggled and Joe rolled his eyes at Chris and shook his head.

A while later, Chris and Jamie had just driven into Riley when his cell phone rang. It was Annie.

"Hey," he answered. "What's up?"

"I can't find my phone charger," she said. "I thought it was in my purse, but it's not there now. I spilled a bunch of stuff out of it in a restaurant earlier. I thought I got it all, but now I'm not sure. There is also the possibility that it is still plugged in in my bedroom. Could you please go check in my room for me?"

He sighed. "Yes, I can do that, but you do know that you are a space case, don't you?"

"I know," she answered. "I really appreciate everything that you do for me."

"I would certainly think so," he replied. "We are on our way back from dinner," he said. "I will call you in a little while."

"Thanks, Chris. Love you."

"Love you too. Bye."

"I guess we are headed to our house to look for Annie's charger," he told her.

"It would seem so," she answered.

"It's not that big of a deal because Barneys need to be let out anyway," he said, "but I didn't tell her that."

A few minutes later, they entered the Wilson home. For some reason, Jamie found the house eerily quiet. Any other time that she had been in the home, she had felt the welcome of the family, but tonight something felt different.

Barney was anxious to get out, so Chris let him out the back door, and then Jamie followed him up the stairs. He switched on the hall light at the top of the steps, and she immediately noticed something. There were several doors in the hallway and every one of them was closed.

He continued walking until he reached the next to the last door. After opening it he turned the overhead light on and walked over to the bed, where the charger lay all by itself. He shook his head and then took a picture of it and sent it to Annie.

Jamie looked around and said, "This is a cute room, but it is certainly small, isn't it?"

Chris nodded and walked over to a door in the corner of the room. He opened it and revealed a very small closet, which was jam packed with clothes.

Jamie was somewhat confused. "Aren't there other bedrooms up here?"

Without saying anything, he motioned for her to follow him. Out in the hall, he opened the door to the next room. He then turned on a light to reveal a very large bedroom which contained a huge bed, which was at least queen or possibly king sized. There was also an enormous dresser containing quite a few good-sized drawers. He then opened another door which revealed a very spacious walk-in closet. Jamie glanced into it and noticed quite a few men's shirts hanging in there.

She looked at Chris. "Did you leave some of your clothes here when you moved over the garage?"

He shook his head. "None of these clothes are mine."

A sudden realization came to Jamie and a cold chill passed through her. "Are they...Kyle's?"

Chris nodded silently.

Jamie then looked around and noticed a wallet and a cell phone lying on the dresser. There were also a few dollar bills and some loose change lying near the wallet.

"Nothing has been touched since the day he died," Chris said quietly. "The only exceptions would be that the things on the dresser were returned to us from the funeral home, and I suppose Mom washed whatever clothes of his that were dirty and placed them back in their proper places."

"It's been like..."

"Well over ten years," he answered.

Jamie looked at him and saw the pain on his face. "This is very...."

"Unhealthy?" he asked.

"I was going to say strange, but I think maybe unhealthy is a better description. I'm guessing that your mother is the one who doesn't want anything touched?"

"Yes," he told her. "The subject is not open for discussion. Of course, Dad who is caught up in his own silent grieving, backs her up."

Tears came to Jamie's eyes. "I feel so bad for them. They are in such terrible pain, but they need to let go of this. It's just ...like a monument to their grief."

"I know," he said. "Wouldn't this make a great room for Annie?"

"It certainly would," she agreed.

"I don't know how many times Annie has begged Mom and Dad to clean out this room and let her move into it, but like I said, it's not allowed to be discussed."

239

Jamie frowned. "Isn't there another bedroom up here?"

He nodded. "My old room is at the other end of the hall, but it has been turned into an office space. There is a guest room downstairs, but Mom wants to keep it open because we usually have Granny stay over at Christmas, and she can't go upstairs."

After a moment, Jamie expressed another thought. "This is about more than just not wanting to let go of Kyle. This is also about the big secret, isn't it?"

"I think so," Chris answered. "It is a multi-layered issue."

"It is also a very sad situation," she said. "I'm sure he wouldn't want it to be this way."

"Absolutely not," he agreed.

Jamie walked over to the dresser and stared at the items lying quietly in a sad sort of manner. She reached out and touched the wallet, and just as she did, there was a power surge or something, because all of the lights went out and then about five seconds later, they came back on. Then

240

whether it was real or imagined, there was a sudden drop in temperature in the room.

Chris and Jamie exchanged a look, and he said, "I think it's time to go."

"Yes," she answered. "I think it is."

Back downstairs, Chris opened the door, and Barney bounded back into the room. The two of them exchanged a look.

"Let's go back to your place," he suggested.

"I think that's a good idea," she agreed. "What about Barney though?"

Chris stared at him. "What do you want to do, you crazy dog?"

Barney stood up as if to say, "I'm ready. Let's go."

A short time later, Chris, Jamie, and Barney were all in Jamie's kitchen eating ice cream. It seemed just the right thing to do to shake off the eeriness of the events that took place at the Wilson home a short time earlier.

Chris laughed and said, "After what happened a little while ago, I swear if I see that rocker move, it's going out on the porch."

Jamie giggled. "The rocker doesn't bother me anymore. Granny said to let it do its thing, so I do."

"I think when we visit Granny tomorrow, we need to get a little more direct with her about Kyle," he said.

"It can't hurt," she told him and then she stood up and picked up their empty ice cream bowls and put them in the sink. Then, noticing that Barney was done, she retrieved his also.

Chris followed her over to the sink and when she turned around, he pulled her close and began to kiss her. At first it was a sweet soft kiss, and then it deepened into a more passionate kiss. After a moment, he pulled away and they exchanged a long look. Eventually, she smiled at him and took his hand and began to lead him into the other room.

"Good night, Barney," he said as they passed through the living room on the way to the bedroom. "Be a good boy. We'll see you in the morning."

The next morning, Jamie sat at her table, drinking coffee, and re-reading the note that she found in front of the Keurig. Her heart warmed thoroughly as she read his words again.

Jamie, I'm sorry, but with everything that happened last night, I forgot to tell you that I needed to get up early this morning to go check on Annie's horse. She seemed a little listless last night and I may have to run to town and get some antibiotics for her. You were sleeping so peacefully that I hated to wake you. I will be back no later than mid-morning. As you have probably figured out by now, I took Barney with me.

I also wanted to tell you that last night was the most incredible experience I've ever had with a woman. I just can't stop smiling. You have come to mean so much to me. I just hope and pray that you feel the same. I can't stop thinking that the future seems bright for us. Be back soon.

Chris

Jamie then went back to her room and got her phone. Back in the kitchen, she took another sip of coffee and sent him a text.

"Good morning. I found your note. Right back at you. My heart is full. See you soon."

It was another hour before Chris returned. It was getting close to the time that they would need to leave to take Granny for her appointment, so Jamie was dressed and ready to go. Chris also appeared to have cleaned up. She was in the kitchen, when he came in through the door that she had left unlocked. As soon as he came in, they exchanged a very loving hug and kiss.

After the kiss ended, he looked at her and said, "I love you, Jamie. I kept wanting to put it in the note, but more importantly, I wanted to say it the first time in person."

She let out a little laugh. "I love you too. I almost put it in the text, but I had the same thought as you. It does seem important to say it out loud."

He kissed her again and then said, "We should probably get going. Granny will be waiting."

"Yes, she will," Jamie answered. "I'm ready."

A little while later, the two of them took Granny to lunch at Applebee's and then they dropped her off at her hairdresser's.

Following that, they went grocery shopping, trying to decide what to fix Granny for dinner that night. Eventually, they decided on fried chicken and mashed potatoes and gravy. Once they finished that shopping, they drove to the pickup area to get the food that Mary had ordered before she left town.

Back at Granny's apartment, the two of them worked on fixing dinner while Granny napped in her chair. They talked quietly about how they were going to approach the subject of Kyle over dinner. They never really came up with a plan, so Chris said that he would just wing it, because you never really could tell where Granny would lead the conversation.

When dinner was ready, they gently woke her up. She then went to the bathroom to freshen up. When she returned, the three of them sat down together and after Granny offered a blessing, they began to enjoy the meal.

Chris finally broached the subject at hand. "Granny could I talk to you about Kyle?" he asked.

"Of course," she answered. "What about him?"

After giving a brief glance to Jamie, he continued by telling her how he had shown his room to Jamie the night before. Then he went on to talk about how Jamie's room needs to be cleared out and that his parents need to let go of his things, so they could possibly move on.

When he finished, she put her fork down and looked at him. "You are absolutely right on all counts, Chris. Your parents do need to let go, but they have pushed their grief and pain down very deep to a place where it is manageable for them."

"Yes, they have," he agreed, "but I think the person who is suffering is Annie. it is not good for her to live around all that. She isn't stupid. She sees things and she has to sleep in that tiny room next door to the shrine to Kyle."

Granny then went into one of her trances. When she finished, Chris spoke again. "I'm sure this is not what Kyle would want."

"It isn't," Granny said. "He is not happy about this situation at all. He wants the best for his daughter."

"Was he with us in his room last night?" Chris asked her.

Granny smiled at him. "I think that you know the answer to that question."

Jamie was sitting quietly listening to this exchange, not completely surprised, but what the woman said next shocked them both.

"Now I am going to tell you something very important and I want you to listen well. I am getting older, and I won't be around forever, you know. However, what you haven't figured out yet is that my abilities have been passed on to someone already. The person who shares the same gifts as me isn't quite ready to be open with them yet, but the time is coming soon that they will need to use them to resolve the situation that you are concerned about."

"You can't tell me who it is?" Chris asked.

"No, my dear," she answered. "The two of you need to figure that out for yourselves."

"The two of us? Do you mean Jamie and I?" he wanted to know.

"Yes," she told him with a smile, "and everyone is very pleased about the two of you expressing the fact that you are in love with each other."

"Are you talking about everyone on this side of life or on the other side?"

Granny smiled. "I would say that it is a mutual feeling on both sides," she told him. There was then a knock on the door and Granny spoke again. That will be my girl here to help me get ready for bed. "Why don't the two of you clean up and then we will have some of those delicious looking brownies before you leave."

An hour later, Chris and Jamie were on their way back to retrieve Barney and head back to her house for the night. They spent most of the ride quietly, each contemplating Granny's surprising speech.

As they stood in the backyard waiting for Barney to finish his business, Jamie looked at Chris and said, "Who do you think that she was talking about?"

He looked at her and said, "There is only one person that I can think of."

"Annie?"

He nodded. "Looking back over the last few years, it kind of makes sense."

"Like her playing matchmaker with us?" Jamie asked.

"Yes. Remember Granny said a while back that you were sent here as part of a plan?"

"I remember that day well," she said. Then she smiled at him. "Can we just table this whole thing for now and enjoy the rest of the night?"

He returned her smile and reached out and pulled her over to him. "I think that we can manage that."

The following evening Chris was watching the Packers game on TV in his parents living room, and Jamie was stretched out with her head on a pillow which was on his lap. She remembered watching the kickoff at the beginning of the game and then she heard something about a two-minute warning.

Suddenly she heard Chris speaking and someone else was answering him. She opened her eyes and realized that Jake, Mary, and Annie had returned. After sitting up, she said, "I thought that they wouldn't be home for another hour."

Chris laughed. "You slept that hour away."

Annie giggled. "She wasn't the only one. You were snoozing pretty good yourself. You two must have had a busy weekend."

"We did," Chris said as he yawned. "We had dinner with Joe and Leslie Friday night. Then we spent the day with Granny yesterday and fixed her a home cooked meal. Today we cleaned the house and did all our laundry."

"You did laundry?" Mary asked with a laugh.

"Well, Jamie managed most of that, but I ran the vacuum cleaner and cleaned the kitchen," he told her.

"I can't tell you how much that pleases me," Mary said with a huge smile. Then she looked at her son. "Please, please, be good to this one. She is a keeper."

Chris looked at Jamie and leaned over and kissed her on the cheek. "You are right Mom. She is definitely a keeper."

Then Annie spoke up. "Jamie isn't going anywhere." Then she picked up her duffle bag and headed up the stairs. Chris and Jamie then exchanged a look, both remembering Granny's words of the night before.

The next month passed very happily. Chris and Jamie managed to spend as much time together as they possibly could. They had dinner together a couple of times through the week and often spent time with Joe and Leslie on the weekends.

It didn't take long for Leslie to learn that the young kindergarten teacher was single, just as she had suspected. However, Leslie was still working on a plan to get to know her better, so she could evaluate whether "Sara" would be a good match for Eddie. Jamie just laughed to herself and decided to leave this project to her friend, because she had enough things going on in her own life.

By the middle of November, Jamie was ecstatically happy. Not only did she love Chris, but she loved his family, her job, and her life in general. Thanksgiving was coming the following week and she couldn't wait for the day to arrive.

Mary was planning to have a large group of family and friends for dinner on Thanksgiving Day. Jamie spent quite a bit of time with her, helping to narrow down the menu and marking who was bringing what and even making a time schedule for that day. It also warmed her heart to know how happy that made Chris.

When the day arrived, everything went smoothly. Jamie enjoyed every minute of it. She couldn't remember a time in her life when she was happier. The next day was black Friday and she got up early and went shopping with Mary. They were able to get a fantastic deal on a Cricut for Annie, which pleased them both very much.

While they were eating lunch, the subject of Annie came up. Jamie got the feeling that Mary really wanted to talk about her, but she wasn't sure why. They discussed some of the things going on in her young life, including her hatred of cheerleaders. Lacey had not made the squad, and they thought that might put an end to it, but she still often mentioned how stuck up and mean cheerleaders could be. There seemed to be no explanation for it.

Then Mary suddenly changed the subject. "Jamie, has Chris talked to you about Kyle?"

"He has," she answered. "He told me what happened to him, and I know that he still misses him."

Mary was quiet for a moment and then asked another question. "Did he tell you anything else about him?"

Jamie sighed and decided that she needed to be honest. "If you are referring to the fact that he was Annie's father, yes I know about that."

"I suppose that you think that I am an awful person for keeping this secret," she said.

"Chris and I have discussed how terrible it would be if she accidentally found out, but Mary, it is not my place to judge you," she said. "I cannot even imagine being in the position that you are in."

"I appreciate you saying that," she replied. "There isn't a day that goes by that I don't think about telling her, but I just don't know how."

Jamie smiled at her, and some words came to her out of nowhere. "I think you will know when the time is right, and I think that Annie is a stronger little girl than you know."

Mary smiled at her. "Thank you. I needed to hear that today."

The rest of the weekend passed quietly. On Sunday afternoon, Jamie was in the Wilson's living room with Chris and the rest of the family watching a football game, when her phone began to ring. She was surprised to see that it was her mother, so she knew that it must be important. Because it was noisy in the room, she took her phone into the kitchen to take the call.

"Hi Mom. What's up?"

"Hello dear. I'm afraid that I have some bad news. Aunt Vera passed away yesterday morning."

"Oh Mom. I'm so sorry. What happened?"

"According to Uncle Vic, she just had a sudden massive heart attack and dropped over dead," her mother explained.

"That's terrible," she answered. "He must be devastated."

"I didn't talk to him long, but he seemed to be holding up well."

At that point Chris entered the kitchen because he had sensed that something was wrong. She had the phone on speaker, so it didn't take long for him to catch up.

"Have they made any arrangements?" she asked.

"Yes, that is why I am calling. There is going to be a viewing next Friday evening from 5 -7 and the funeral is on Saturday at 10:00. Do you think you might be able to get a flight? Maybe you could get one of those discount airlines. That's what I'm doing."

"Is the funeral home in Norwood?"

"Yes."

"I don't know Mom. I'll have to check. You know they only fly in and out of certain cities on certain days. It might be better to drive, but I'm sure it would take at least six- or seven-hours to get there from here. I'll have to get back to you."

"Well, honey, I'm sure that they will expect to see you there."

"Like I said…hold on a second." Chris was motioning to her.

"What?"

"I'll see that you get there. I will drive you."

"Chris, that would be three days of your time," she said.

"I don't want you to go alone. Please let me do this."

Jamie held his gaze for a moment and then went back to her conversation with her mother. "Mom, I will be there. I'll call you later with the details."

After she finished her call, she looked at him and grinned. "You do realize that Norwood is a suburb of Cincinnati?"

"I looked it up when I heard you ask about it," he said. "It doesn't matter. I love you Jamie, and I want to take care of you."

The two of them then stood in the kitchen holding each other for a moment before they returned to the living room walking hand in hand.

Chapter Ten

Chris and Jamie departed from her house around seven o'clock the following Friday morning. Within the hour they had gone through Madison and were traveling on I-80 toward Chicago.

As she always did when traveling on long car trips in which she was a passenger, Jamie had brought a pillow with her. Not long after they had passed through Madison, she felt herself drifting off to sleep.

At some point later, Jamie realized that Chris was talking to someone on his phone. She had no idea who was on the other side of the conversation, but it was easy to see that whatever the person was telling him was making him happy.

"That is great news," she heard him say. "Can we get on that the first of next week?"

There was a pause and then he said, "I guess that I can understand that. My original thought was to tear the house down and build a new one, but where it is currently sitting is not the most ideal location anyway. I guess it could stand until sometime in the future."

After another moment of listening, he concluded the call. "All right buddy. I'll call you Monday morning."

He looked over at her. "Well, good morning sunshine. Welcome back to the land of the living."

Jamie smiled at him. "Are we close to Chicago?" she asked.

Chris laughed. "Sweetheart, you slept through Chicago. We are in Indiana, halfway to Indianapolis. It's almost eleven o'clock."

"Oh my. I'm so sorry," she said. "I haven't been very good company, have I?"

"No need to apologize," he told her. "You have had a hectic week. I'm sorry that the phone woke you, but that was an important call that I didn't want to miss."

"Was that about the farm that you are interested in buying?" she wanted to know.

"Yes," he said with a smile. "That was the grandson of the old couple living there. I went to school with him, and I let him know a while back that I might be interested in buying the farm. Sadly, the wife took a fall and broke her hip, so they won't be able to stay there alone anymore. An arrangement has been made for them to move into the same senior living place that Granny lives in. Anyway, his parents told him to contact me and set up a meeting with them."

"What was that about the house?" she asked.

He sighed. "Apparently, they do have one condition concerning the sale. They want the house to remain intact as long as the old couple is alive. I guess that they have lived there for their entire married life. He said they may want to drive

259

them by it once in a while and it would break their hearts if it were torn down."

"Ahhh," she said. "That is so sweet."

"Yeah, I guess it is," he replied. "Like I was telling Devon, it's not that big of a deal. There are some other better places to build." A moment later, he continued. "I could use a break. The next exit looks like it has several places to eat. Let's stop and have an early lunch."

"That sounds good to me," she answered.

It was around 3:25 when they arrived at the Ramada Inn where they had reserved a room. Jamie had texted her mother and she was waiting for them in the lobby. At the sight of her mother, a sense of happiness flooded over Jamie, and she realized that she had missed her more than she had admitted to herself.

The two of them exchanged a warm hug and then she turned to Chris. "Mom, this is Chris Wilson, who was kind enough to drive me all the way here. Chris, this is my mother, Sharon Barnes."

"It is nice to meet you," Chris said.

"It is very nice to meet you too," Sharon told him. "I can't tell you how much I appreciate you bringing her here; not just for the funeral, but we haven't seen each other in about nine months or so, and I've missed my daughter."

"It was my pleasure," he told her and then after smiling towards Jamie he continued. "She has become very important to me, and I certainly didn't want her to make this trip alone."

Sharon took a long look at her daughter before speaking. "Shall we get you checked in? We will probably need to leave in about an hour or so."

The two hours of viewing time seemed to drag on and on to Jamie. After expressing her condolences to the immediate family. She sat with Chris in the back row of chairs that were set up in the viewing room. Most of the people that came in were strangers to her, but various distant family members came to speak to her one by one, so she repeatedly introduced Chris to them and told the story of her move to Wisconsin. Since Vera was Sharon's sister, she stood near the front greeting people who came in to express their condolences.

Many of them were familiar to her because she had grown up in the area.

When the viewing time was thankfully over, Jamie began to worry that they would be invited to go eat at a restaurant or someone's home. She hated to be rude, but she was tired from the trip, and she could tell that Chris was worn out too.

Blessedly, that did not happen, so Chris, Jamie, and Sharon returned to the inn and decided to have dinner right there in the restaurant. While they ate, Sharon asked Chris about the farm and what kind of crops and animals they raised. The meal was good and when they finished, Chris let out a subtle yawn and announced that he was going upstairs to retire for the night. Jamie was sure that he was tired, but she also understood that he was giving her an opportunity to spend some time alone with her mother.

When he was gone, Sharon looked at her daughter and smiled. "He seems very nice. I like him. Is this serious?"

Jamie couldn't help but smile at her mother's question. "We haven't been together a very long time, but I think that it is moving in that direction."

"Well, I already like him much better than Craig," she answered, "but I guess that is no secret that I didn't care much for him. So, how did you meet Chris?"

"His mother is the guidance counselor at my school," Jamie told her. "My house isn't far from their farm and his little sister Annie's dog kept running to my house. He liked one of the previous residents and I think he is still looking for her. Anyway, Mary told me to text her whenever he showed up and Chris would sometimes come over to get him. Then Annie started spending time with me because she liked working with the Cricut, and Chris would pick her up sometimes too. Eventually, we started going out as friends and then we became more than that." Jamie didn't think it was necessary to tell her about the amount of time that they spent researching dead people. It was the kind of thing that made sense to the two of them, but if you said it out loud, you might get some strange looks.

"I hope it works out, honey," she said. "You seem very happy around him."

Jamie smiled, because she was pleased that her mother was interested in her life, so she decided to return the favor. "Are you excited about your cruise? Tell me about it."

At the mention of the cruise, Sharon's face fell. "Unfortunately, that is not going to work out," she said.

"Oh, no. What happened?" Jamie wanted to know.

"Well, the first thing was that Marie's husband that she was separated from was diagnosed with stage 4 cancer, and she felt an obligation to stay home and take care of him after his surgery and during his chemo sessions. Then Marsha was in a car accident, and she has a broken clavicle and a badly bruised knee. The two of them were able to get their money refunded on medical exemptions. That left Patty and me, and truthfully, the two of us have never really been on that friendly of terms, so I really didn't want to go anymore, but I was stuck with it because I had a non-refundable deposit tied up in it. Last week, Patty called me and said that her sister was willing to buy my trip, so I jumped on it; problem solved."

"I guess," Jamie said, "but now you have no plans for the holidays."

Sharon smiled at her. "True, but I've been thinking about how I hung you out to dry when I was all into my plans. I felt kind of bad about that, and now I think that karma has come to bite me in the butt."

"Maybe we can work something out," Jamie told her.

"Oh no. I wouldn't dream of asking you to miss the holidays with Chris."

Jamie thought for a moment. "Maybe you could come to stay with me for a few days."

"That's very nice, but I don't know if Chris's family would want a stranger hanging out with them during Christmas," Sharon answered.

Jamie grinned. "You haven't met Mary. She is extremely family oriented, and if she gets wind of this, she won't let up until she knows that neither of us will be alone on Christmas."

"She sounds like a wonderful person," she said. "Let me give it some thought and check into the flight situation."

"Fair enough," Jamie told her, as she let out a yawn. "I need to get to bed myself. By the way when are you going back?"

"I have a flight out tomorrow at 3," she answered. "If I didn't take that one, I couldn't get another on Allegiant or Frontier until Tuesday and I have no desire to stay around Vic that long."

Jamie giggled. "Another person that you are not fond of, for good reason, I am sure."

Sharon gave her daughter a direct look. "You don't even want to know."

"No, I don't," she replied. "Let's head upstairs."

Back in the room, Jamie found Chris sound asleep in bed. She tried to be as quiet as possible while she went through her nightly routine. Then she slid into bed and curled up next to him while trying not to wake him. Whether he was awake or not, she didn't know, but he put his arm around her and pulled her close. Jamie soon drifted off into a happy dreamless sleep.

She woke to the feeling of someone gently shaking her shoulder. "Jamie it's 6:45. Aren't we supposed to meet your mother for breakfast at 8?"

Jamie opened one eye and then the other. "I think we have found the one possible issue in our relationship."

He laughed. "What? That I am a morning person, and you are...not? If that is your only character flaw, I can forgive you for that." Then he whacked her on the bottom before saying, "Let's go!"

That got her up and headed toward the bathroom. On her way across the room she said, "That is far from my only flaw."

"What else have you got?" he asked.

Just before she shut the bathroom door, she called out. "I'm going to leave that a mystery for now."

Jamie was relieved that the funeral service only lasted about twenty minutes. As the three of them waited in Chris's truck for the funeral procession to begin moving, Jamie noticed Chris checking something on his phone.

"If you don't mind me asking, why do you keep looking at your phone? Is something wrong at home?" Jamie asked him.

He sighed. "The weather system that is moving up toward northern Indiana and Wisconsin seems to be picking up speed and momentum. Now it looks like there is not only snow but some ice moving ahead of it. I planned to leave right after the lunch that their church is putting on, but I think we need to skip that and head on out."

"I hope this doesn't mess up my flight," Sharon said.

"No," he told her. "You will be way south of the system. I just want to be sure to be home ahead of it. It does look nasty." Then he turned around to her. "Do you still want us to take you to the airport, or do you want to stay for lunch and beg for a ride or take a cab? It's your call."

"Hmm," she said. "This is a dilemma. I hate to have you go out of the way on my account, but on the other hand, I really dread going to lunch. I am very tired of hearing about poor Vic when I know how badly he treated my sister."

Jamie turned around and smiled at her mother. "We'll take you."

Chris looked at the rearview mirror. "It will be fine. Let's say our good-byes at the cemetery."

An hour and a half later, Chris and Jamie dropped Sharon off at the departure terminal of the Greater Cincinnati International Airport. She promised her mother that she would update her with texts to let her know that they remained ahead of the storm.

It didn't take long for them to drive I-275 and connect to I-74 which would lead them to Indianapolis. They stopped just north of that city for a quick lunch and then went on their way toward Chicago.

Around three-thirty, there was a noticeable change in the weather. The sky grew darker, and the temperature dropped. While they were stopped at a roadside rest, Jamie noticed a chill in the air and when she stepped back outside, a cold rain had begun to fall. She began to feel a little anxiety over the situation. She didn't say anything to Chris, but she noticed that he had grown quieter and was more focused on the road.

About twenty minutes later, an overhead digital sign indicated that there had been an accident twenty miles ahead and traffic was stopped. A couple of miles down the road, traffic slowed to a crawl and the rain was coming down harder.

Chris looked over at her. "It seems we have a choice. There is an exit coming up. We can take it and try to get around this mess, or we can stay on the interstate and hope we are not stranded for hours."

Before Jamie started to speak, there was a noise on the windshield. It was the sound of ice hitting the glass. "We are getting off this highway," Chris decided. "We may just have to look for a place to stay to wait the storm out."

"I think that sounds like the best idea," she said. "I don't want to sit here for hours."

A few minutes later, they took the exit and began to move at a crawl on the road that was now ice-covered. Neither of them said a word. Chris was focused on the road and Jamie didn't want to distract him.

They had crept along for about forty minutes at the speed of around thirty miles an hour, when they miraculously came upon a small gas station that was open. Chris pulled into their parking lot, put the truck in gear and looked at her. "This is not good. We may have to just spend the night here in the truck. I know that doesn't sound pleasant, but it's better than going on and sliding off the road and nobody being able to get to us."

Jamie stared at him for a moment. "I guess that I have to trust your judgement. The only thing that worries me is what kind of neighborhood this is," she said as she looked around."

Chris then lifted the lid off the console that was between them to show her the handgun that was placed there. Jamie simply nodded at him, and he closed it and the two of them walked inside the little store that was part of the station.

"Hello," the man working the counter said to them. "What are two nice looking people like you doing out in a storm like this?"

Jamie then realized that they were still dressed in the clothes that they had worn to the funeral. Chris smiled at the man and then explained to him where they were traveling to and asked him if they could spend the night in the parking lot.

"You can stay here if you want, but I can tell you that there is a Motel 6 about five miles down the road," he told them. "I'm not sure if they will have any rooms on a night like tonight. I guess that you could call and ask."

Chris looked at Jamie and said, "What do you think?"

She nodded at him. "At least call and find out and then we can decide."

The man looked up the number for Chris and he called and spoke to them. He looked over at Jamie. "They have a couple of rooms left. Do you want to go for it?"

"It's fine with me," she said, "but it is your call."

Chris looked at her for a moment and then gave the person on the phone his credit card number. Then the two of them loaded up on drinks and snacks, because they didn't know what was going to be available at or near the motel.

Ten minutes later they were on their way. They drove in the direction that the man had told them to go. Neither of them spoke because the road that they were on was very dark and the freezing rain continued to fall. When they had been driving about fifteen minutes, they had to go down a hill and there was a bridge with guardrails on both sides at the bottom.

It seemed to Jamie that when they were at the top of the hill, Chris paused for a moment and Jamie sensed that he was possibly praying. As they went down the hill, Jamie did not want to look at the road, so she stared into the woods off to her right. Just as they were about to reach the bridge, she saw a bright light flashing in the woods. The strange thing was that it was not at ground level, but up high in the trees.

She opened her mouth to say something about it, but as soon as the truck reached the bottom of the hill, it began to slide and they turned around in a complete circle twice, hitting the guardrail on each side. Somehow, they managed to get across the bridge and once they were on the other side Chris was able to gain control of the vehicle.

Once he had done that, he looked over at her. "Are you all right?" he wanted to know.

She nodded. "As soon as my heart stops pounding, I'll be fine."

He gave her a small smile and said, "Let's get out of here."

The rest of the drive to the motel was slow but uneventful. When he finally pulled up to the front of the motel, she said a prayer of thanks.

"Go on in," he told her. "I'll park and bring our bags in."

Twenty minutes later, Chris unlocked the door to their room. After the light was flipped on, the two of them stood and stared at the room for a moment. There was one double bed covered with an outdated looking flowered bedspread. Next to that was a small table with two chairs. There was a single window that looked out on the back parking lot.

Chris looked at Jamie and smiled. "It might not be a five-star room, but it is definitely a step up from my truck."

"True that," she answered. "By the way, did you check out the damage to your truck?"

"No, I didn't," he said.

"I feel terrible about that," she told him.

He then stepped over to her and wrapped his arms around her. "Jamie, it's a truck. It can be repaired or even replaced if need be. My only concern tonight was you."

Jamie melted into his arms and then remembered something. "Chris, just as we were sliding down that hill, did you happen to see…."

"The flashing lights?" he asked.

She nodded. "What did you think about that?"

He shrugged. "Maybe it was a warning?"

"Possibly," she answered, "or was it a sign that everything would be all right?"

"I suppose it could have been," Chris said. "I guess we'll never know for sure."

Jamie reached up and gave him a kiss. Then she walked over and took a good look at the bed. After a moment, she pulled back the bedspread. "I don't see anything too nasty. I guess it will do. I'm hungry. Let's dig into the snacks that we bought."

A little while later, Chris found a college football game on TV, so he stretched out on the bed to watch it while Jamie took a shower. When she came out, she was feeling refreshed, but Chris had fallen asleep. She laughed to herself thinking that this was the second night in a row that she had come to bed to find him asleep.

However, when she slid into bed next to him, he reached over and pulled her close and they then shared the most passionate lovemaking that they had experienced so far. Jamie fell asleep almost immediately afterward, dreaming of Chris and a large, beautiful house.

She woke up several hours later to the sound of the shower running. Looking over at the bedside clock, she saw that it was 5:15. Confused, she sat up just as she heard the shower turn off. A moment later, Chris came out of the bathroom. Seeing her sitting up he said, "Sorry that I woke you, but I was going to anyway. I couldn't sleep well, because of worrying about the weather, so when I woke up at 5, I saw that we have a window between the end of the freezing rain and the beginning of the snow."

"I see," she answered. "More fun driving."

"Come on, sleepy head," he told her. "Let's go. If you hurry, we can grab some breakfast." That was enough to motivate her.

To Jamie's delight, they did find a Waffle House that was open right next to the interstate entrance ramp. Once they were full of coffee and food, they again set out for Chicago.

They made it through the city with no trouble, but as soon as they passed through the outskirts, the snow began to fall, and travel became slow again. However, they were now on the interstate, the sun was coming up and it wasn't as frightening as the night before.

It was noon when they arrived in Riley and Jamie couldn't have been more relieved. Chris called his mother and spoke to her through the Bluetooth on his radio.

"Hey," he said. "We are just coming into town. Do you have power?"

"No," she answered. "We are on generator. The ice took down a whole lot of trees."

"Ok. Do you need anything as we are coming through?"

"We're good," she told him. I saw this coming and stocked up yesterday. Are you bringing Jamie here with you?"

"I am," he said. "We'll probably make a quick stop at her house and then we should be there in thirty minutes or so."

"Great. I have vegetable soup on the stove. See you in a few."

"Bye."

He looked at her and smiled. "The trip from hell is almost over."

Jamie sighed. "And not one minute too soon."

The stop at Jamie's house didn't take long. Jamie grabbed up some more clothes and then made a quick call to John and Carol letting them know the power was out and that she was going to stay at the Wilson's. They weren't surprised and then they asked her to turn off the water so the pipes wouldn't freeze because the temperature was expected to drop below freezing overnight.

A little while later, they were sitting at the table in the Wilson's kitchen eating soup with Jake and Mary. As they ate, they related the adventure of their long trip.

"I feel terrible for dragging him into this mess," Jamie said. "Now his truck is all dented and scratched." Then before he could say it again, she continued. "I know it's just a truck."

"Well, I have to take part of the blame," he said. "I never should have gotten off the freeway in the middle of a winter storm."

Jake who was usually a man of few words now spoke up. "I was just going to ask you what the hell were you thinking doing that?"

Chris shrugged. "I guess that I was worried about us being stuck in a traffic jam for hours. I don't know whether that would have been worse than ending up in a seedy hotel room or not. Anyway, we're here safe and sound. I guess that's the main thing."

After studying his son for a moment, he spoke again. "I know your tired, but I do need your help in the barn for a few minutes."

Five minutes later, Jamie was alone with Mary. She looked around and asked a question.

"Where is Annie?"

279

Mary sighed. "She is in her room, and she is not a happy camper.

"Why? What has happened now?"

"One of the girls that made the cheerleading squad got hurt and broke her arm or something, so they went to the next girl on the list and invited her to join the team."

"Lacey?"

"Yep," Mary nodded. "And we are right back to the cheerleaders are snobs drama."

"I wish we could figure out why she has this vendetta against cheerleaders," Jamie said.

"I don't understand it," Mary answered. "She has never known any cheerleaders that I know of." She was quiet for a moment. Then she said something that Jamie found very interesting.

"Do you want to know something ironic?"

"What?" Jamie asked.

"Her mother was a cheerleader."

"Kyle's girlfriend?"

"Her name was Holly," Mary told her, "but Annie has no way of knowing any of that."

Jamie couldn't respond to that statement because a thought was whirling around in her mind. "No, surely not," she thought. "It couldn't be."

Then Mary suddenly changed the subject. "I've been thinking about Christmas. It's going to sneak up on us."

That reminded Jamie of the conversation that she had had with her mother, and she related the whole story to Mary, who said, "Of course your mother is welcome to join us for Christmas. Let's just take a moment to figure this out. You don't have an extra bed in your house, do you?"

"No, I don't," she answered. "That does present a problem for me."

"Well," Mary explained, "my original thought was to put Granny in the guest room as usual and I thought that you and Chris could sleep in his place, and we would all be here Christmas morning."

"You wouldn't care about me staying there with Chris?" Jamie asked.

"Oh please," she said. "You two are adults and we're not stupid. Anyway, I'm planning on the two of you sleeping in the guest room tonight because his apartment isn't hooked to the generator and there isn't anywhere else left in the house."

There was then an awkward silence because they both knew that was not entirely true. After a few seconds, Mary again shifted the subject.

"However, yesterday when we were at Granny's, she wasn't doing too well. She seems to tire more easily lately. Jake and I were discussing that maybe we should go visit her Christmas Eve and then if she is up to it, we could bring her here for dinner the next day. I think an overnight might be too much for her. Then we would have a room for your mother."

Jamie thought for a moment and then remembered something. "You know when Chris and I were there last weekend, she said something about her not being around forever. How old is she?"

"She will be ninety-two in January," Mary told her. Then a sad look came across her face. "If she is talking about not being here, then I guess that we should prepare ourselves."

"As sad as that is, I think you may be right," Jamie replied.

Then Mary turned to her and said something else that surprised her.

"Jamie please don't mention this Christmas room arrangement to Chris until I get it worked out." She paused and then continued. "I just can't deal with him pressuring me about Kyle's room right now."

Chapter Eleven

The power came back on around 8:30 Monday evening. Mary insisted that Jamie stay one more night because her house would take a while to warm up and Chris and Jamie had beaten her and Jake at Euchre several times in a row and she felt a comeback coming soon. School had already been cancelled for Tuesday, so she didn't put up any argument. Besides, she wasn't going to turn down an opportunity to spend another night with Chris.

She kept her promise to Mary and didn't discuss anything with him about the arrangements for Christmas, nor did she say anything concerning her thoughts about Annie's mother being a cheerleader. It wasn't hard to keep her thoughts to herself because Chris and Jake had been busy making sure that the cows were safe during the storm. This was the first night that the two of them hadn't been outside late.

Annie had not been very congenial over the last few days. However, on Monday she went from sulking to only being quietly indifferent. Jamie considered attempting to talk to her about the situation, but she was afraid she might be overstepping her bounds. Jake, Mary, and Chris seemed to be ignoring her pouting, so she decided to do the same.

By Tuesday morning, there was 4 inches of snow on the ground. Most of the power in the area had been restored, so a call was put out on the system that school would resume on Wednesday. Jamie had mixed emotions about going back to school. She had enjoyed this little break, but she knew that the longer her students were out of school, the harder it would be to get them back into a routine. Besides that, there was only one week now before the Christmas break began.

By the end of the day Thursday, Leslie was all excited because she had accomplished her goal of fixing up the young kindergarten aide, Sarah, with Eddie. They were going on a completely blind date the following Saturday night. Jamie was amused by how proud her friend was of herself, but she decided to remain out of the situation in case it came crashing down around them.

The next weekend Chris and Jamie went to see Granny and they could see what Mary was talking about. While she seemed happy to see them, some of the sparkle seemed to be gone from her eyes. Later that night, when the two of them reported back to Jake and Mary, the four of them had a discussion and it was decided that Granny would be brought to the house on Christmas Day, instead of staying overnight on Christmas Eve.

The following school week was only three days long and then the Christmas break would begin. By the end of the day Tuesday, Leslie was beside herself wondering how the blind date went. She had not been at work on Monday because she had a follow-up appointment for her ankle, and she had not seen Sara the entire day.

"Has Chris talked to Eddie?" she asked Jamie.

"If he has, he hasn't said anything to me," she answered, but he has been kind of busy lately, at the barn and then he has had some meetings in town." Jamie did not want to go into details about the fact that Chris was about to purchase a 250-acre farm.

Leslie grinned at her. "Could you please try to find out from him?"

Jamie was about to respond when her cell phone that was lying on her desk jumped to life and announced that Chris was calling. She sighed inwardly and answered it.

"Hi," she said. "I am still at school. Leslie and I were just talking, and you are on speaker."

"Hey Leslie," he said.

"She was just asking me if I knew whether you have talked to Eddie this week," Jamie told him.

Chris laughed. "As a matter of fact, I did run into him earlier today."

Before Jamie could respond Leslie jumped into the conversation and asked, "Did he mention anything about how his blind date went last weekend?"

Jamie could feel Chris grinning because they had discussed the situation the night before. "Well Leslie, as a matter of fact he did tell me that he had a really nice time, and he said that he was planning to call her sometime in the next few days and ask her if she would like to go out again this weekend."

"That is fantastic," Leslie said as she lit up like a Christmas tree. "Joe told me that I was being silly about the whole thing, but I feel like there is something there." Then she stood up and said, "I better get back over to my room and start packing up."

When she was gone Chris and Jamie had a laugh over her antics. Then he said, "The reason that I called is that I forgot to tell you that I have a Cattlemen's Association meeting tonight in town, so I probably won't be over."

"That's fine," she answered. "I have several things to do to get ready for tomorrow, since it is the last school day before Christmas." Then after a moment of thought, she continued. "Maybe I will see if Annie would like to come over and help me. She would probably be better help to me than you with wrapping presents and baking."

Chris let out a laugh. "You are one hundred percent right about that," he told her. "I've got to get off here. I need to get my barn work done before I go tonight. I'll call you later."

"All right," she said. "I love you."

"Love you too," Chris said.

Jamie then stood and picked up a couple of papers off her desk and headed toward the office. Her plan was to make some copies and then drop into Mary's office and ask her about Annie coming over.

When she arrived at the copier, Mary and Sandy were there and the machine was opened, and they were attempting to clear a major paper jam. Jamie took one look at the situation and said, "My copies can wait until morning." Then she asked Mary about having Annie over for the evening.

After looking up, Mary replied. "It's fine with me. She rode the bus here and is in my office doing something on my computer. You can take her with you if you want. I may be here a while."

Jamie went on down the hall to Mary's office. Surprisingly, the door was closed. As she opened it and stepped in, Annie had a strange reaction. Jamie could not see what was on the screen of the computer, but she had the definite impression that Annie was quickly attempting to close whatever browsers that she had open.

"Hey kiddo," she said. "What are you up to?"

Annie's face turned a very slight shade of red, but she smiled and said, "Nothing much. I was just fooling around on the computer until Mom is ready to go home."

"I could use some help tonight getting ready for the party day tomorrow. I talked to your mom, and she said that she was going to be awhile, so would you like to come home with me? We could get some pizza before we go."

The girl's face lit up at her invitation. "Sure. Let me ask Mom if it's ok," she answered.

"She already told me that it was fine," Jamie said. "Get your things and we'll tell her bye on the way back to my room."

An hour later, the two of them were eating pizza. Jamie was asking her some general questions about school hoping to learn what the status of her friendship with Lacey was. Annie didn't mention anything about Lacey, but she did refer to a new girl that she had struck up a friendship with. Her name was Angie, and she had just moved into the area from somewhere in the northern part of the state. Then Annie made a point of telling her that the two of them had a lot in common; most importantly that Angie was not the cheerleader type.

Jamie came very close to coming right out and asking the child to explain why she hated cheerleaders so much, but there was a knock at the door, and it was Mary. They had invited her to stop and have some pizza because Jake was going to the same meeting as Chris and food was going to be served there.

Mary stayed for a while and the three of them had a good time talking and laughing. Then

291

she headed home, and Jamie put Angie to work wrapping the gifts that she had purchased for her students. Jamie mixed up cupcake batter and when they were in the oven, she went to help her finish.

"What did you get Chris for Christmas?" Annie wanted to know.

"Hmm," Jamie responded. "If I tell you, how do I know that I can trust you?"

"Well," Annie replied. "I know what he got you."

"Do you now? He didn't tell you, did he?" Jamie asked her, finding that a little hard to believe.

Annie giggled. "No, of course not. I am just a good sneak."

"Well, I'm not," she answered. "I like to be surprised, so I have never been a sneak; even when I was a kid."

Annie wasn't sure where to go with that information, so she was quiet for a moment. "So, I guess that you are not going to tell me what you got him?" Annie eventually asked.

"No," she told her. "I don't think so. It's not that I don't trust you, it's just that I still might take it back and get a different kind or something else altogether. I still have time."

"Hmm," Annie responded. "That is interesting. You have now piqued my curiosity."

Jamie smiled. "Well, your curiosity is just going to have to wait until Christmas.

With a sigh, Annie gave up on her gift quiz and changed the subject. "When is your mother coming?"

"She is flying in on the 23rd," Jamie told her.

"It's nice that your mother is coming," Annie said. "Everybody should be with family at Christmas. Now you don't have to be sad about your mother not wanting to be with you."

Jamie looked over at the girl and noticed a sad look come across her face, and the thought once again entered her mind that they were all missing something that was going on with this child. However, her gut instincts were telling her to leave things alone for the time being. Then the timer went off on the oven and she decided to let things be.

A couple of hours later, she drove Annie home and then returned to her house just before Chris called. He was just leaving Valene, and he asked about her evening, and she gave him the general details, but the same instinct that told her not to ask Annie what was going on told her not to talk to Chris just yet. Somehow, she had the feeling that she should not stir the pot before Christmas.

On the 23rd of the month, Chris and Jamie went to the airport in Madison to pick up her mother. Sharon's flight had been delayed and then there had been quite a bit of turbulence in the air, so she was very happy to arrive, although Jamie sensed that she was a little nervous about staying with people that she had never met.

Her anxiety did not last long because Mary was in full holiday mode, and she soon made her feel quite at ease. Jamie smiled to herself as she could see the potential for the two women to become friends.

The final arrangement was for Sharon to sleep in the guest room, and Chris and Jamie were going to stay at her house, because it wasn't that far, and he stayed there most weekends anyway.

Granny had not been feeling well enough to go to the hairdressers for the last few weeks, so when the subject came up, Sharon volunteered to go to her apartment and wash and set her hair. She had been a beautician and had run her own shop for many years, and she said that she would just need to go to Walmart and pick up some supplies. It was settled then that the first thing in the morning, Mary and Sharon would set out on a mission to fix Granny's hair.

As Jamie left with Chris shortly after that, her heart was full. Never in her life had she felt so loved by so many people. Something told her that Chris was feeling the same way. When the two of them went to bed that night, they were simply happy to curl up together and drift off to sleep.

The next day was Christmas Eve and Granny was happy to have her hair done, but when it was finished, she declared herself too tired to go anywhere or have visitors on Christmas Eve. She just said that she would rest up for Christmas Day.

On Christmas Eve, the Wilson's, and Sharon, gathered for a dinner made of various finger foods such as wings, shrimp, meatballs, cheeseballs, and a variety of sweets that Mary had been baking for days. Around seven, they went to a candlelight service at a church in town. When they returned it was time to open the gifts.

Although Jamie had declared herself a lover of surprises to Annie, she was now very curious to see what Chris had bought her for Christmas. It was the Wilson family tradition that instead of passing out the gifts to those who were receiving them, each person went to the tree and gathered the gifts they were giving. Then one by one, each person took a turn personally presenting their gifts to the person who was receiving them.

When it was Chris's turn, he handed a large box to his mother. Inside of it, was a beautiful leather bag for her to use as a school bag. Her smile indicated that she loved it, but when Jamie glanced at Annie, she was wearing a look of total confusion. Chris laughed and said, "You are not quite as smart as you think that you are."

Then it was Jamie's turn. She stared at the gifts sitting at her feet and decided to just go right to her gift for Chris. After handing the box to him, she sat back and waited somewhat nervously. When he pulled the leather jacket out of the box, he couldn't have been more surprised or pleased. A month earlier, they had been to the mall, and they had happened to pass a store that had some leather jackets displayed near the door. Chris had stopped and looked at them and he commented on how he had always thought about buying one, but he just never wanted to spend the money. He told her with a smile that he hadn't given it another thought since that night, but he was thrilled that she had remembered.

Chris's gift for Jamie ended up being the very last gift of the evening. The box was a small rectangular one. The obvious thought was that it was jewelry, but Jamie was fairly certain that it was not.

Once she opened it, she had to go through a few layers of tissue and at the very bottom of the box there was what appeared to be a couple of tickets. Jamie lifted them out and then smiled at him. "These are tickets to see Journey."

Chris nodded. "I know they are your favorite band. You need to read the fine print, though."

Jamie looked down at the tickets. "The concert is in March," she said.

"Look again," he told her.

Her eyes flew open wide. "This concert is in Sarasota," she exclaimed.

"Yes, it is," he said. "It's during your spring break. You mentioned something about going down there, so I thought that we could go together and take in the concert. I have the plane tickets and your mother said that we could stay with her."

Jamie looked over at her mother. "You knew?"

"I did," she answered.

At that point, she couldn't contain her smile. "Thank you," she said. "I can't wait."

"Neither can I," he grinned.

"Ok, enough gooey stuff," Annie said. "Jamie, are you going to help me set up my new Cricut tomorrow?"

"I'd be happy to," Jamie answered. "It might be after dinner, but I promise I'll find some time."

"I'm hungry," Jake then announced. "Let's get the food back out."

A couple of hours later, Chris and Jamie returned to her house and then they sat up for another couple of hours talking about the future, and how they hoped that this was the first of many Christmases together.

The next day was quite busy with making preparations for the big dinner. Around noon, Jake and Chris left to go get Granny. When they returned with her, both Mary and Jamie noticed how tired she already looked. It made Jamie sad, because she knew that Granny was beginning to slip away.

Dinner was a pleasant affair. One of Mary's sisters came with her husband, so they had quite a large group. Once the meal was over, and the table was cleared, there was another round of gift giving and when that was over, they all enjoyed pumpkin pie for dessert.

Mary could see that Granny was running out of steam and when she asked her if she was ready to go home, the woman nodded quickly.

When Jake said that he would pull the car around, Granny perked up for a moment and requested that Chris and Jamie take her. Jake shrugged with a confused look and then agreed.

An hour later, they had Granny settled in her chair. Chris had called the number to let her aide know that she was home and ready for her to come and get her into her bed.

While they waited, the woman seemed to come to life for a few minutes. "I wanted to speak to both of you about Annie. She is struggling through some things right now. The girl thinks the world of both of you and you will need to be there for her when the time is right."

The two of them exchanged a look. Then Jamie spoke. "We have all been concerned about Annie, but we are not sure what is going on. I've been wanting to talk to her, but something is telling me to hold off."

"And your instincts are correct," Granny told her. "This is something that she must work through herself. She will tell you when she is ready." She paused for a moment and then continued. "There is a cycle of things that need to happen, and I'm afraid I won't be here to see it all through, so I am passing that job on to the two of you."

Chris spoke next. "Is Annie the one that has your gift?"

"There are many of us who can enjoy the gift if we are open to it," she said, looking directly at Jamie. "When you feel a strong instinct, listen carefully, because it may be an important message."

Again, Chris and Jamie looked at each other and then there was a knock at the door and the aide walked in.

"I'll say good night now," she said. "Thank you for making this a pleasant Christmas. You two take care of Annie and each other."

They were both quiet on the return trip to the farm. Eventually, Chris tried to break the dark mood that hung over them. "I'm looking forward to the dance on New Year's Eve. It should be fun. I don't think that I even mind getting dressed up."

Jamie looked over at him and smiled. "I'm looking forward to seeing you in a suit."

"It doesn't happen often," he told her. "Consider this a special occasion, because I usually only break out a whole suit for weddings and funerals."

"Oh, that reminds me," she said. "Guess what I got in the mail today."

"I have no idea," he answered. "Was it money?"

Jamie laughed. "No, but it is something that could potentially cost me some money. I received an invitation to Lisa's wedding."

"Are you serious?" he asked. "Are you going?"

"Well, the ornery side of me considered accepting and then asking you to go with me just to frustrate Lisa, because I'm sure she hasn't given up reuniting me with Craig. Then I looked at the invitation again and I realized that there was no plus 1. It was to me and me alone, so I marked decline on the invitation and sent it back with no regrets."

"Are you going to send a gift?" he wanted to know.

"I haven't decided yet," she responded. "If I do it will be the least expensive thing on her registry or possibly just a gift card."

"By the way," Chris said," I forgot to tell you. Eddie is taking Sara to the dance, so that will provide us with a side show watching Leslie monitoring the situation."

Jamie giggled. "I know. Sara told Leslie and we are all going shopping for dresses on Tuesday."

"Well, I don't know about how this girl feels, but Eddie seems to like her," Chris told her.

"According to Leslie, she is into him, but it's possible that she is reading too much into the situation because her hopes are high. I'll know more after our shopping day."

The day at the mall did turn out to be fun. Jamie decided that she liked Sara. The girl wasn't quite as young as she had initially thought. She was in her mid-twenties like the rest of them. When Jamie learned that she lived at home with her parents because her mother was almost legally blind, and her father was suffering from arthritis, she felt an immediate bond with her. When she told Sara that she had been through a similar situation with her parents, the two of them made an instant connection.

The dance that the six of them attended was held at a hotel in Madison. They had all reserved rooms ahead of time, so they were able to get ready at the hotel. There was a buffet dinner at seven and the band began to play at eight-thirty. Jamie was happy to see that Chris was a good dancer and he seemed to enjoy himself on the dance floor. The time until midnight passed quickly and at ten forty-five a curtain on one wall was pulled back and a ceiling projector showed the scene in New York City as people prepared to watch the ball drop. Madison is in the central time zone, so they all watched the ball drop at eleven and then they celebrated the New Year again at midnight. It was a fun evening, and at midnight Chris kissed Jamie and then spoke seriously to her.

"I love you, Jamie, and I have a feeling some great things are coming our way."

"I love you too," she answered softly. "I can't wait to see what this year will bring for us."

The next day, the six friends had breakfast together in the hotel restaurant before heading their separate ways. Leslie was happy because she felt that her matchmaking was a success. Eddie and Sara just seemed happy to be together, and

Chris and Jamie were still in the glow of their declaration of a future together.

On the way home, Chris and Jamie picked up Annie from her friend Angie's house where she had spent the night. The child seemed quiet on the way home and Jamie's concerns about Annie were renewed. She couldn't help but pray that she hadn't had another falling out with a friend.

Later that day, they all enjoyed a pork roast and sauerkraut dinner. When dinner was finished, they all sat around and talked about the fact that they had enjoyed the holidays, but they were glad that they were over. Jamie looked over at Chris and wondered if she was sure that she felt that way. The two of them had spent every night together since Christmas Eve and she wasn't sure how they were going to manage to go back to their pre-holiday routine. He looked over at her and she could feel that he was thinking the same thing.

At that point jake then asked if anybody would like to share any New Year's Eve resolutions. It was quiet for a moment, and then Mary spoke.

"I have one," she began. "This school year has been difficult for me so far. I think that you all know that, but I have been carrying my school problems around and letting it drag me down. I need to stop that. That's not fair to the rest of you. From now on. I'm going to check my school issues at the door."

"I'm happy to hear that sweetheart," Jake told her. "That will not only benefit us, but it will be good for you too."

"What about you?" she asked him. "Do you have any resolutions?"

Jake shook his head. "No, I'm happy with my life just the way it is."

They all laughed and then Mary said, "I love you, honey."

"Anybody else?" Jake asked, looking at his son.

Chris looked over at Jamie. "I'm not necessarily going to make a resolution, but my life has been changing for the better lately, and I'm going to do everything in my power to see that the good things continue to happen."

Jamie smiled back at him and simply said, "Ditto."

Annie then lit up for the first time that afternoon. "If you get married, dibs on being in the wedding."

That night Chris stayed at Jamie's house again, which made her happy. It wasn't discussed, he just went home with her. The following day was the last day before school resumed. The day was cold with a mixture of rain and snow. Chris asked her what she wanted to do, and she told him that she would like to stay home and curl up with him and some blankets and watch movies on TV. He stayed that next night too, and it was a good thing because he practically had to roll her out of bed in the morning.

Once she got to school, she was happy to see her kids and it seemed easy to roll into the second half of the school year. At the end of the third day back, she was in her room, packing her bag to go home, when Mary appeared at her door. It was obvious from the look on her face that something was very wrong.

"Mary. Has something happened?"

"I just got a call from the nurse at Granny's facility," she said in an almost croaky voice. "Her aide went in to check on her this afternoon. She found her in her chair asleep and she couldn't wake her up. They have taken her to the hospital."

Chapter Twelve

Jamie shivered as an icy cold wind blew across the cemetery. Two inches of snow had fallen the day before, but the sun was now shining, which seemed to make the fresh fallen snow appear to glisten. The minister was still giving his final blessings over the casket which contained Granny's body.

For some unknown reason, Jamie was compelled to look over at the top of the hill to her right, and what she saw surprised her. There was a beautiful deer standing there looking down at the scene. This seemed strange to her for a couple of reasons. She was used to seeing deer in the summer in wooded areas, but more often than not, they scattered at the sight or sound of human activity. This deer, however, was staring right down at the scene of the funeral.

Her next compulsion was to look at Annie, who was sitting in the row in front of her next to Mary. The child had also noticed the deer and was staring at it with a smile on her face. Jamie's next surprise was that Annie turned and looked back at her. Their eyes locked for a moment. Then a few seconds later when the minister said, "Let us pray", Annie turned back around and bowed her head. As Jamie did the same, she had the strange feeling that she may have just witnessed something mystical. As soon as the minister said, "Amen", she looked back up at the hill to see that the deer was gone.

A couple of hours later, they were all back at the Wilson home. The table was spread with the many dishes of food that had been brought in by a multitude of friends and family. Some of

Jake's family had come to the house after the funeral as well as a few close friends.

Mary looked as if the days since Granny's death were about to get the best of her, so Jamie was trying to help as much as she could. At one point, she went into the kitchen to make more coffee. She was alone in the room, until Annie entered. The girl came and stood next to her, but she didn't speak right away.

Jamie smiled at her. "I don't know about you, but I'm about ready for these people to go home."

"For real," she answered. "I'm getting tired of people asking me how I'm doing." Then after a moment she spoke again. "You saw it, didn't you?"

After she finished counting the scoops of coffee that she was putting in the filter, Jamie answered her. "If you are talking about the deer, yes, I did see it. It was beautiful, wasn't it?"

Annie frowned and was quiet for a moment before she responded. "It was." Then she turned and left the kitchen without another word. Jamie stared after her, feeling that once again she was missing something. Then she sighed and finished making the coffee.

After Granny's death and funeral, life was quiet and calm for Jamie and the Wilson's. Annie's mood seemed to perk up a little. Her friendship with Angie continued, but there was still no mention of Lacey, which made Jamie sad because it indicated that she was still harboring her dislike of cheerleaders.

The relationship between Chris and Jamie continued to grow. While he didn't stay every night at her house, he did stay every weekend and at least one or two nights through the week. He didn't seem to want to discuss the subject of Granny or who she had been talking to, so she decided to give him some space on the issue for the time being.

One thing that she didn't mention to him was that the chair was suddenly more active. On several occasions, she was certain that she saw it move out of the corner of her eye. She also had to push it back in its place a few times, because the tape marks weren't lined up.

On the Wednesday of the third week of January, Jamie was in her room after school with Leslie. They were discussing an email that had been sent out from the principal earlier that afternoon. It informed them that there would be a staff meeting after school on Friday. This meeting was mandatory for all teachers and support staff.

"This is very strange," Leslie told her. "As long as I've worked here, there has never been a staff meeting on a Friday afternoon. Something tells me that this is not good news."

"What makes you think that?" Jamie wanted to know.

"Well, the Friday afternoon thing is suspicious," she explained. "The best way to give bad news to people is right before the weekend. Then you can send them home so that they can cool off before Monday morning."

"I suppose," Jamie said, "but it could just be that was the only time that worked."

"No," Leslie answered. "Something is going on. Have you noticed that John Newsome has been spending a lot of time around here lately?"

Jamie shrugged. "I don't know. I really haven't paid that much attention."

"Well, I have," Leslie replied. "I've seen him walking around with a group of men a couple of times and they were all carrying clipboards."

Jamie laughed. "Leslie, I think you've missed your true calling. You should have been a writer."

As it turned out, Leslie's intuitions were more correct than either of them could have foreseen. By Friday afternoon, the rumors that were flying through the school were too numerous to keep track of. All the employees assembled promptly, because they were anxious to learn the subject of this important meeting. John Newsome wasted no time delivering his message.

"First, I would like to apologize for delaying the start of your weekend. I will come straight to the point. As you all know this building is quite old and has more than its share of ageing problems. Over the last few years, we have made every effort to repair as many of these problems as possible, to keep this building operational. It is no secret that the district is in the sixth year of a ten-

year plan to build a new elementary school just outside of Valene, and when that happens, Riley Elementary will be closed.

However, in recent months some new issues have come to light that is causing us to alter that plan. At the beginning of last month, the local health department inspected our sewage system. At that time, they discovered that the system is operating in an unsafe manner. Their initial report to the school board indicated that the school should be closed immediately. After some discussion and negotiating, the health department has agreed to allow the building to stay open until the end of this school year.

Now obviously the big question is what will happen next year, because there is no possible way that we can have a new building up and running by the next school year. I won't go through all the details, but after several meetings and a good deal of research, the board has arrived at a decision. We are going to merge this building with the elementary building in Valene. This will be done by purchasing several modular classrooms which will be placed behind the current building. This obviously will be a temporary situation. We are also working to speed up the process of constructing the new building. At this time, we hope that the new elementary will be ready for use after two more school years.

I know that all of you are wondering how this will affect each of you personally. I can tell you that the situation during those two years will be different. Class sizes will be larger. Some of you will have changes in your teaching positions. I'm sorry, but there is no way around that. You do have my word that seniority will rule. Over the next few weeks, I will be meeting with each of you to discuss your assignment for next year. Thank you for your time and enjoy your weekend."

Jamie walked back to her room without waiting for Leslie, Kim, or Gina. There were three words ringing in her ear. *"Seniority will rule."* She couldn't help but think about the fact that she was the last one hired. All she wanted to do was go home and try to process what she had learned.

Just as she stepped out into the hallway, she heard someone call her name. She turned and was surprised to see John Newsome walking in her direction.

"I'm glad that I caught you before you left. Can we talk for just a few minutes?" he asked her.

"Of course," she answered and stepped back into her room.

John followed her and closed the door behind them. Then he smiled at her and spoke. "I know that you are probably concerned because you are our most recent hire, and I want to put your mind at ease as best as I can at this point."

Jamie had absolutely no idea how to respond to his words, so she just waited for him to continue.

"First, I want to let you know that I have reviewed all the evaluations that Tom has written about you so far, and both of us could not be more pleased with the job that you have done." He let out a small sigh and then continued. "At this point we do not have a specific assignment for you. However, we do have a few teachers that are eligible for retirement. We are making plans to offer them some enticing incentives to go ahead and retire. There are also some other options that we are looking into. I'm sorry I don't have a specific placement for you right now, but I want to assure you that we are going to make every effort to have you under contract next August. Then if for some reason, it doesn't work out, You have my word that you will be the very next person hired; if not in the next two years, then definitely when the new building is opened."

From the expression on his face, Jamie could tell that he was being sincere, and that he did not enjoy the position that he was in. She smiled at him and then responded to him.

"I understand that this is a complicated situation, and I appreciate the effort that you are making for me."

He let out a small laugh. "Complicated is an understatement. By the way, I was prepared to tell you not to worry over the rent for the house next fall if things don't work out, but after the call Carol got from Chris earlier this week, I guess you may have a new landlord by that time anyway."

Jamie frowned at his remark, but before she could say anything, John's phone rang. He looked at it and said, "I need to take this call. I'll be in touch." Then he left the room and headed back up the hallway.

Since she was still holding her bag, she went on out to the parking lot and headed home. By now, her head was nearly spinning with information overload. Right at the top of her mind was the question, *"Was Chris trying to buy the property that her house was on without even mentioning it to her?"*

Just as she was getting out of the car in her driveway, her phone rang, and it was Chris. For some reason, she decided not to answer it. Instead, she just let it ring and went on into the house. In the living room, she dropped her bag on the couch and headed into the kitchen to get herself a glass of tea.

Twenty minutes later, she had changed into sweatpants and a T-shirt, and she was sitting on the couch with her feet on the coffee table. Looking over at the chair she said, "Don't you have anything to say today?" For once it was unresponsive.

It wasn't long before Chris pulled into the driveway and then a minute later, he walked in the doorway. He stood there a moment staring at her. "Are you alright?" he asked her. "I thought we were going to get Chinese tonight."

Jamie sighed. "Oh sorry. I guess I forgot."

"You seem upset," he said. "Did something happen at school?"

"Yes," she answered. "We had a bomb dropped on us this afternoon."

"What?"

Jamie then told him about the meeting and John's big announcement, and her conversation with him in her room.

"That is a kick in the butt," he replied, "but it sounds like they are going to make every effort to keep you employed."

Jamie nodded. "I think they are going to go after Bessie pretty hard, which I have mixed emotions about. She needs to retire, but I do feel sorry for her."

"The whole situation is kind of a mess, isn't it?" he asked.

"It sure is," she said. "Things could get rather strained."

Chris stared at her for a moment. "There is something else, isn't there?"

At that point, she sat quietly trying to decide how to approach the subject of the property. When she didn't respond he said. "Talk to me Jamie."

"John mentioned something about me not worrying about the rent because of a phone call that you made to Carol, and that I might have a new landlord next fall." Then she looked directly at him. "Chris, are you trying to buy this property?"

He let out a sigh. "I was going to tell you about that this weekend. I only called her yesterday. My idea was to put the original farm back together. Are you upset with me because I didn't tell you?"

"I'm not necessarily upset," she told him. "I am just surprised that since I live on this property, you didn't mention it. I guess what you do with your money is your business."

Evidently her words caught him off guard because he didn't answer right away. Then his next words surprised her. "You are in a mood, aren't you?"

Now the frustrations of the last few hours came to a boiling point and Chris received the brunt of it. "I'm not in a '*mood*'. I just found out that I may have lost my job, and that my home is being sold out from under me. I have to take care of myself Chris. I don't live on my parents' property, and I don't work in the family business. I am on my own."

As soon as the words were out of her mouth, she knew that she had made a mistake, but it was too late. She watched the anger come across his face and a few seconds later, he stood up and stormed out of the house. She didn't look out the window, but she heard the sound of the truck door slamming and his truck spinning out of the driveway.

An hour later, Chris went into the house looking for his father. He found his mother in the kitchen. She told him that Jake had driven Annie into town to Angie's house. Then he was going to talk to the manager of Granny's apartment complex to make arrangements to clean out her things.

"He was hoping to do it next Saturday," she said. "Can you be available?"

"Sure," he answered.

Then she looked at him and frowned. "It's Friday night. Aren't you going out with Jamie?"

"No," he told her. "I guess not."

Mary stopped cutting potatoes and turned to him. "Is Jamie upset about the meeting this afternoon?"

Chris nodded. "She's in quite a state."

"She's so upset that she wants to be alone?"

He sighed. "I was over there. We had a little disagreement, so I just decided to give her some space."

"Is she worried about losing her job?" she asked.

"John tracked her down after the meeting and told her that they didn't have a position for her right now," he said. "He also told her that they were going to put the pressure on a couple of teachers to retire."

"Bessie for one?"

"She thinks so," he answered. "Then John let it slip that I called Carol and asked her if she would consider selling her grandmother's property to me."

"Hmm," she replied. "I gather that you hadn't mentioned that to Jamie.

"I was planning to talk to her about that this weekend," he said. "It was just unfortunate that John inadvertently mentioned that to her when she was already upset about the job situation."

"Did she get angry with you about not telling her?"

He sighed. "At first she was just kind of annoyed, but then I made the mistake of saying that she was in a bad mood."

"Ooooooh you didn't."

He nodded his head. "Then she gave me a speech about how she wasn't in a bad mood; she was upset because she was losing her job, and her home was being sold out from under her. After that she went on to say that she had to take care of herself because she didn't live with her parents and work in the family business."

"How did you respond to that?" Mary wanted to know.

At this point, Chris felt a little sheepish. "It made me angry, so I just left."

"You felt attacked?"

"I did," he answered.

324

Mary went back to her potatoes and then after a moment, she spoke again. "Chris, she may not have picked the best moment to express her feelings, but I think she may have a point. I know you work hard here, and the farm is better off for your work, but you have never been in the position that she is in. You have always had us to fall back on. I'm not saying that that is a bad thing, but it's not the same as having to depend solely on yourself."

"I get that," he said. "What made me angry was that the last thing that she said was that she was on her own. Why would she say that? We've talked about the future, and how we hoped to be together for a long time. I just don't get why she would feel that way."

"Well, son, I don't know for sure," she told him. "Maybe you need to ask her about that. You know it's easy to talk and dream about the future, but sometimes real life can come crashing into your dreams. Could it be that it is time to stop talking and start planning?"

Chris considered his mother's words and then he leaned over and kissed her on the cheek. "Thanks Mom," he said and then turned and walked out of the house.

After having quite a good cry, Jamie eventually fell asleep on the couch. When she woke it was dark outside. For a few minutes, she lay in the darkness, feeling very alone. Her heart hurt for Chris, and as she replayed the words that she had said to him in her mind, she felt terrible. As the tears threatened to flow again, she got up and went into the kitchen. After she switched on the light, her eyes went to the clock on the stove. It was seven forty-five.

She opened the refrigerator and stared at it for a moment. Nothing in there appealed to her, so she closed it and opened the pantry. Nothing in there jumped out at her either. Then before she could decide what to do next, there was a knock at the door. For a moment, she froze. It had to be Chris. A little voice inside of her said, "*Go open the door, you fool*."

When she opened it, he was standing there looking about as upset as she felt. "Can I come in?" he asked. "It's kind of cold out here."

Jamie let out a small grin and stepped aside. "Sure."

Once he was inside, he closed the door and then turned back to her. "We need to talk, but there is one thing that I want to say first. I love you, Jamie. I love you very much."

The tears then fell freely as she said, "I love you too. I'm really sorry for what I said. That was uncalled for."

He then pulled her into his arms and held her tightly. They stood that way for several minutes and then he pulled away slightly. "We need to talk," he told her. Then he motioned her over to the couch.

Once they were settled, he began. "I'm sorry too for running off like that. I guess I was just stunned by what you said, but after I had a chance to think it over, I realized that you had a point. At least the part about having to take care of yourself. I've never really been in that position.

What bothered me the most was when you said that you were alone. Jamie, honey, you are not alone, and you never will be as long as I am around. We've talked about the future and sharing it together, but I guess maybe, talk can be cheap. Maybe it's time to stop talking and dreaming about the future and start putting a plan into place if you are ready to do that."

Jamie looked at this man that she loved so much and smiled. "I'm yours. You've owned me since day one."

He smiled back at her. "Will you marry me?"

"Absolutely. Just name the time and place."

Then he reached into his pocket and pulled out a small box. He flipped it open and pulled out a diamond ring. "I bought this about two weeks ago. I was waiting for the right time. I don't think there could be a better time than right now." Then he slid the ring onto her finger.

She looked down at it and said, "It's beautiful. I couldn't have picked a better choice myself."

Chris pulled her close and they shared a deeply passionate kiss. A few minutes later, he said, "Do you know what?"

"What?"

"I'm really hungry," he said.

Jamie laughed. "So am I."

"Chinese?"

"Give me a few minutes," she said. "I must look a mess."

"How about we call in an order and I just go pick it up?" he asked. "I think I would like to have you all to myself tonight."

Jamie's heart swelled with love. "I'm all yours."

As they hugged one more time, neither of them saw the chair begin to rock.

The next morning, the two of them walked hand in hand into the Wilson home. They found Jake and Mary eating breakfast in the kitchen.

"Is there anything left?" Chris asked. "We are hungry, and Jamie's cupboard is kind of bare."

"There is no cooked food left, but you are welcome to fix your own," Mary told them.

About fifteen minutes later, the two of them sat down with their eggs, toast, and coffee. As they ate, they kept looking at each other and smiling.

"Do the two of you have something that you want to share with the class?" Jake asked.

Jamie glanced over at Chris, and he nodded at her. Then she held up her hand and wiggled her fingers. Mary gasped and then immediately began to cry. "This is so ...exciting...wonderful and a whole lot of other words."

"We do have a plan," Chris said. "After some discussion, we mutually agreed that we want a very small wedding, very soon. We are going to see Reverend Baker at the Methodist Church in town and see if we can have a small wedding there sometime in the next few weeks, depending on how soon we can get Sharon to fly up here. We are thinking that it will just be our family, Leslie, and Joe, and maybe Eddie. Then we will reserve a room in a restaurant for a dinner."

"It sounds perfect," Mary said. "If that's what you want."

"I'm not into the big wedding thing," Jamie told her. "To be honest, I think it's a big waste of money."

Mary laughed. "You are preaching to the choir, dear. Jake and I eloped and never regretted it."

"Were your parents upset?" Jamie asked.

"My parents were relieved that they didn't have to pay for a big wedding," Mary answered. "Granny, of course, claimed she knew about it before it happened."

They all laughed, and Jamie's heart overflowed once again.

Two weeks later, Jamie stood in front of a full-length mirror looking at herself in her wedding dress. She had selected a tea-length dress with a long-sleeved lace covered top and a pleated skirt. In her hair she wore a simple flower. Her mother, Mary, and Annie stood behind her; all admiring her dress."

"You look beautiful," Annie told her.

"You know when you first said that you didn't want a full-length dress, I was kind of disappointed," Sharon said, "but looking at you now, I can see that this is the perfect dress for you."

"Yes, it is," Mary said. "My only regret is that Granny isn't here."

Jamie smiled. "I think that she will be. She kind of gave us her blessing when we took her home on Christmas Day."

"She did?" Mary asked.

"Yes," Jamie answered. "She told us to take care of each other."

"Hmm," Mary answered. "If that's what Granny said, then that's what you will have to do."

"That is exactly our plan," Jamie said.

"Good," Mary told her. "Because I'm done doing his laundry."

The four of them had a good laugh over that.

Thirty minutes later, Chris and Jamie exchanged wedding vows in front of a small group of family and friends. It was a short but poignant ceremony. When it was over, the group travelled to a restaurant in Valene that had just opened. It had a private party room in the back.

They had selected a choice of prime rib or chicken and several choices of side dishes for their guests. The food was absolutely delicious, and everyone seemed to thoroughly enjoy themselves.

When the meal and the celebration were over, the two of them returned to Jamie's house, where they planned to live until their new house was built, hopefully, by the end of the year. Since they already had a trip planned over her spring break, they decided that that would be their honeymoon.

When they walked in the front door, they both stopped and stared. The chair was in the middle of the room. "I guess whoever sits and rocks in the chair was so excited about the wedding, that they rocked their way clear across the room."

Chris did not answer her, but he simply pushed the chair back where it belonged. Then he held his hand out to her and led her to the bedroom. Jamie giggled and took his hand. The activities of the chair bothered him a lot more than it did her.

Much later that night, they lay in bed talking about many things. At one point the subject of Annie came up. Jamie decided that it was time to tell Chris that she thought that it was possible that the girl had learned the truth about her real parents.

Chris thought for a moment. "I guess that I had forgotten that Holly was a cheerleader. I remember now that she was totally into it. She always had to look exactly perfect. Kyle use to laugh about it."

"I can think of several ways that she might have learned that Kyle was her father, but I wonder how she would have known about her mother being a cheerleader?"

"I have no idea," he answered. "That certainly is a missing piece of the puzzle."

"We could ask her, but I keep remembering Granny's words that she is working through it, and she will tell us when she is ready," Jamie said.

"There is another consideration here too," he told her.

"What is that?" she asked.

"Mom...and Dad."

"Oh yeah. We don't know how they are going to take it when they find out that she knows the truth."

"Of course, this is all speculation at this point," he said. "We are just assuming that she knows."

"That is true," she answered with a yawn.

Chris then yawned himself and as he pulled her closer to him, he said, "Good night, Mrs. Wilson."

Out in the living room, the chair began to rock, slowly this time. A peacefulness settled over the house as they slept in their home.

Two weeks later, on Saturday morning, the Wilson's were all gathered in the basement of the Wilson home staring at a large group of boxes that were stacked in a corner. Inside the boxes were Granny's personal belongings. The family had decided to donate her furniture, housewares, and clothes to the facility for any residents who might be in need, so they had only brought back her small items.

After a moment, Jake spoke quietly. "Mary and I have agreed that there is nothing of Mom's that we need or want. So, the three of you can go through these things and either keep them, give them away or throw them out. It is entirely up to you." Then the two of them turned and walked back up the stairs.

Annie turned to Chris and Jamie. "Mom and Dad just aren't into going through dead people's things, are they?"

Chris gave her a serious look. "I think you are absolutely right about that." Then he looked around. "Well, let's get started."

It took them all of that day and several hours the next afternoon to go through the boxes. After everything was sorted, there were three boxes of things that they decided to keep. There was a small amount of jewelry. Among those items, the only thing that was really of value was her wedding rings, which Chris and Jamie insisted that Annie keep.

Jamie was interested to learn that Granny had a passion for dolphins. Apparently, before she became too old and unable to travel, she had taken yearly trips to various beaches in Florida. In her jewelry collection there were several necklaces with dolphin pendants and there was also a bracelet that contained a dolphin charm.

Jamie watched as Annie held the bracelet in the palm of her hand and squeezed it. Then Jamie's heart took a leap as the girl got a look on her face that was very similar to the look that she had seen on Granny's face several times. Then she looked at Jamie and said, "Granny got this the last time she went to the beach. She was planning on adding more dolphins when she went again, but she never went back."

Jamie looked over at Chris who was gathering up some trash bags that needed to be taken out to the trash containers. Apparently, he hadn't heard any of this conversation. Then she watched him head upstairs.

"Did Granny tell you about this bracelet?" Jamie wanted to know.

Annie thought for a moment before she responded. "I guess that she must have," she answered.

Then a moment later, she handed the bracelet to Jamie. "Why don't you take it? You're going to the beach soon. Maybe you can find another charm for it. I think Granny would like that."

Jamie reached out and took the piece of jewelry from her. Somehow when it was in her hand, it just seemed to feel right. She smiled at her young friend and said, "Thank you."

Chapter Thirteen

The wheels of the plane touched down on the runway with a loud screech. Jamie looked out the window and smiled because the sunshine was glinting off everything. When they had taken off from Madison the weather was cold and gloomy, and the forecast was predicting rain and snow for the next several days.

An hour later, they were in a rental car, heading toward a beach condo where they were planning to spend the week. When Chris had first decided to make a Christmas gift of the concert tickets and the trip, Sharon had offered to let them stay with her, but after they decided to get married, Jake and Mary rented the condo for them as a wedding gift. They did, however, plan to spend time with Sharon during the week.

The condo was a ground floor unit that had a small patio and a direct walk out to the beach. Jamie was thrilled as this was her first time seeing the ocean, and she was so delighted with the view that she would have been happy to have spent her entire week sitting on the patio or walking on the beach. The weather was predicted to be perfect through the week, with highs in the low eighties and practically no chance of rain.

During their first morning, they spent the day walking up and down the beach, looking for seashells and splashing around in the ways. During the afternoon, they took beach chairs down to the waterline, where they could put their feet in the water. Jamie read a book, and Chris soon dozed off. Eventually, it became much warmer, and the tide began to move in, so they packed up and returned to the condo, where they made love and then fell asleep in each other's arms.

The next day, they went to a nearby small town that was full of tourist shops. The two of them spent most of the morning strolling through the small stores. They purchased several gifts for family and friends along the way. They were just about to return to the car and look for a place to have lunch, when Jamie happened to notice a small shop called, "Gifts from the Ocean". It was on the other side of the street from the car, but for some reason, Jamie was compelled to walk over to it. "I'll be right back," she told Chris.

Jamie wandered through the shop, not sure what she was looking for, but she had a strong feeling that there was something in the store that she wanted. Most of the items in the shop were somewhat cheesy; mugs and dishes with beachy sayings on them, fake looking shells, and painted signs for beach homes.

Just as she was about to give up, she happened to notice a small jewelry rack on top of a display case. She walked over to it and began to browse through the pieces. There were a few necklaces made from shells and sand dollars and some bracelets. Then suddenly she saw what she believed to be the reason that she had been drawn into the shop. There was a small collection of charms hanging at the bottom of the rack. One of them was a dolphin that was very similar to the one that hung on the bracelet of Granny's that Annie had given to her. There was no price tag on it, so Jamie picked it up and took it to the register.

"How much is this charm?" she asked the clerk.

"Hmm," the lady answered. "I didn't know that we had this. This is my mother's store, and she does all the buying." She thought for a moment and then continued. "Does $14.95 sound like a fair price?"

Jamie smiled and reached into her purse to retrieve a twenty-dollar bill. As she waited for the woman to hand her the change and the charm, she couldn't help but think of Granny. Had she sent her in here? Was that possible?

Outside, Chris had the car running with the AC on. When she got in the car, she showed him the charm and told him about how it matched the one that was Granny's.

"But why did you go in there in the first place?" he asked.

"I have no idea," she answered. "When I saw the store, I just had a very strong compulsion to go in there."

Chris stared at her for a moment. "I have to tell you something. Just before you went in there, there was a look that came across your face that was similar to the looks that Granny used to get. I'm beginning to wonder if maybe you are the one that the gift has been passed to."

Jamie thought about what he said. "The strange thing is that I saw that same look on Annie's face just before she gave me the bracelet."

"Hmm," Chris answered. "Remember that Granny also said the gift was there for anyone who was open to it."

"Yes, she did," Jamie agreed, "and at this point, I'm certainly a believer."

The next evening, Chris and Jamie had reservations at an upscale beachfront restaurant that Sharon had recommended. It wasn't far from their condo, so they decided to walk by way of the beach.

Jamie selected a summery dress that she had purchased on their shopping venture the day before. As she was going through the jewelry that she had brought, looking for earrings, she saw the bracelet with the dolphin charm attached to it. She quickly picked it up and went to the living area of the condo where the bag with the new dolphin charm still sat on the coffee table. A moment later, the bracelet with both dolphins attached was hanging from her wrist. She looked at it and smiled, hoping that Granny was happy.

The two of them walked hand in hand to the restaurant. It was still somewhat warm, but a nice breeze was blowing in from the gulf, so the walk was enjoyable. Jamie's heart was full, but she wanted time to slow down a little because they were just about halfway through their trip.

The food and the service at the restaurant were outstanding. They both ordered a steak and seafood combo, and they were not disappointed. After finishing off their meal with a piece of key lime pie which they shared, the walk back to the condo was welcome.

When they were about halfway back, they stopped to watch the sun drop down into the sky. Just after the orange ball disappeared into the

344

horizon, a dolphin jumped out of the water and did a twist before plunging back in the waves. They watched for a moment longer and were rewarded when two more dolphins repeated the same motion. There was quickly another one appearing and as they watched the show for several more minutes, they later estimated that there were at least three or possibly four dolphins traveling together.

When it appeared that the dolphins had moved on, Jamie touched the bracelet on her arm and smiled. "Message received, Granny. I understand that you are pleased."

The following evening, Sharon came to their condo, and they grilled steaks in a common area that belonged to the building that the condominium was in. It was a nice evening, so they ate at the small table on their patio while watching the sunset again. Jamie kept an eye out for more dolphins, but none appeared.

After they finished their meal, Chris said that he needed to talk to his father about a situation involving their cattle, so Jamie and Sharon decided to take a walk on the beach. They walked quietly for a while and then Jamie told her mother about the dolphins that they had seen the night before. After another moment Sharon asked her daughter a question.

"Chris makes you very happy, doesn't he?"

"Yes, he does," Jamie answered, a little surprised at the question.

"I'm very happy about that," Sharon replied. "I would hate to see you spend a lifetime with someone that you weren't...passionate about."

After a moment, Jamie decided to bring her thoughts out in the open. "Is that what you did, Mom?"

Sharon didn't respond immediately, and she seemed to be considering her words. "Please don't misunderstand me, Jamie. I cared for your father. It was just never a passionate relationship. I know that you sensed that things weren't always the best between us, and they weren't." She paused for a moment and then continued.

"You are an adult now and I think that you deserve to know the truth."

Jamie felt a slight sense of dread come over her, as she braced herself for whatever she was about to hear.

"This story actually goes all the way back to my high school days," she began. "I had a high school sweetheart name Phil Jackson. When we graduated, we were full of lots of grandiose ideas about going off to college together and then getting married. Then his father got a job promotion which transferred him to Colorado. To my complete shock, they insisted that he move with them. To make sure he complied, they refused to financially support him in any way other than their plan and promised him a brand-new car. It was a difficult decision, but eventually he caved to their demands."

Jamie looked at her mother. "You must have been devastated."

"I was." Sharon answered. "I couldn't even think about going to college at all after he left. My parents said that I had to do something, so that's when I decided to go to cosmetology school. Once I graduated, I went to work in a local salon and that's where I met your father. He was one of my clients, and he was kind, and I was lonely and so was he. We dated for about six weeks and then we decided to get married."

"I thought that Chris and I rushed it, but that's really quick," Jamie said.

347

"Within the first six months, I think that we both realized that we had made a mistake, but I don't think that either one of us had the guts to speak up and do something about it."

"So, you just drifted along?"

Sharon sighed. "If only it had been that simple." She took a breath and then continued. "I came to find out that your father had an affair with a woman that he worked with. I confronted him about it, and he was honest. He said it didn't mean anything, which I think was true, but I was young and immature, so I did something that added insult to injury."

Jamie stopped walking and looked at her mother. "What?"

"I went out and had an affair of my own with one of my clients that was always coming on to me."

"You didn't?" Jamie asked. "And I'm guessing you came back and threw it right in Dad's face?"

"I did," she answered. "We then had a horrible nasty argument. When the dust eventually settled, we decided that it was time to go our separate ways."

"What happened?" Jamie wanted to know.

Sharon paused for a few seconds. "You happened."

"You found out that you were pregnant with me?" she asked and then a horrible thought occurred to her. "Oh, please don't tell me."

"The whole time I was pregnant with you, I wasn't sure who your father was," she admitted. "After you were born, your father insisted that we take a DNA test. I agreed because I wanted to know too. When the results came back, I think that your father and I were both happy. Your father is actually your biological father."

Tears of relief came to Jamie's eyes. "So, then you decided to stay together for my sake?"

"Yes, we did," Sharon answered. "Your father adored you. I think if I ever had left him, he would have fought me for custody."

Those words warmed Jamie's heart, and she had a sudden sense of nostalgia for her father.

"Jamie, it wasn't all bad. We had some good times, didn't we?"

After a moment of thought she nodded without comment.

"I think that there was a kind of unspoken agreement, that when you were on your own, that we would go on with our lives separately," Sharon said.

"But then Dad got sick?"

Sharon nodded. "I couldn't leave him alone. I stayed with him because I owed him that much."

"I still miss him," Jamie told her.

"You may not believe this, honey, but so do I," Sharon responded.

Jamie thought for another moment and then asked a question. "Mom, if you had not gotten pregnant with me and you had left Dad, what would you have done?"

After a sigh, Sharon responded. "I wanted to go to school to become a teacher as I had originally planned and try to build more of an adult life than I had lived, and I was also going to enjoy myself."

Jamie smiled. "Is that the reason for the party lifestyle that you have sought out down here?"

"I found out very quickly that the party lifestyle wasn't really for me," she said. "Since the cruise fell apart, things got rather dull around here until just recently."

"What happened recently?" Jamie wanted to know.

"Well, since everybody's lives seem to be an open book on social media these days, I decided to look up Phil Jackson. It didn't take me long to find him. Amazingly, he lives in Fort Myers."

"Is he married?" Jamie asked.

"No, just after he retired from the accounting firm that he had worked for for over forty-two years, his wife left him. I guess it was a long overdue parting of the ways." Sharon replied. "So, like me, he moved down here to start a new life."

"Interesting," was Jamie's response. "Any plans to see him?"

Sharon's face turned slightly red. "He drove up here two weeks ago. We went to dinner, and

we had a nice time catching up with each other."
After a moment, she continued. "In answer to
your next question, we are talking or texting
about every day and I'm planning to drive down
there next Saturday, after the two of you leave."

Jamie thought this over as she began to
walk again. Eventually, she shared her thoughts.
"I'm glad for you Mom. I think you deserve some
happiness."

Later that night, Jamie lay awake as Chris
slept next to her. She had not shared her mother's
story with him yet. Eventually, she would, but she
needed some time to process what she had
learned. A lot of things that her mother had told
her had not really shocked her. She did, however,
have a moment of near devastation before her
mother revealed the results of the DNA test. How
would she have felt if her mother had dropped
the bomb on her that her whole life was a lie?"

Then her mind went to Annie. What
happened tonight with her mother was a small
window into what this girl will go through if she
learns the truth about who her parents really are.
Or what if what Jamie had growing suspicions

about was true, and she was already dealing with the truth. Before she drifted off to sleep, she decided that she needed to have a discussion with Chris about this situation and convince him that it was time to get all the cards out on the table. There was no reason to let the girl suffer alone.

The Journey concert was on Thursday night and just as they were almost ready to leave, Sharon called and told them that Phil had decided to drive up on Friday because he wanted to meet Jamie and Chris. She said that he wanted to take them all out to dinner.

The concert was incredible. The music was so good that they stood through almost the entire event. Jamie couldn't remember when she had enjoyed herself so much. Then it occurred to her that she had said that to herself a lot since she had become involved with Chris.

When they returned to the condo that night, they were too keyed up to think about sleeping, so they ended up sitting on the couch having a general discussion about their life. Chris surprised her by bringing up something that had apparently been on his mind.

"Jamie, we are married now, and you no longer have to worry about taking care of yourself all by yourself. I know that you love teaching and if that is what you want to do, I will support you completely. However, if you are not offered a job for next year or if they offer you something that is not desirable to you, I don't want you to feel like you have to take it because you think that you need to pull your weight. We would be just fine. I guess what I'm saying is that I want you to work if that's what makes you happy, not because you think that you need to. Do you understand what I'm saying?"

Jamie smiled. "I do understand, and I appreciate you telling me that. Why don't we just wait and see what happens and then we will make a decision together?"

"We can do that," he answered. "By the way, Dad told me that Mom doesn't want to go back to work next year."

"She has had a rough time this year," Jamie said.

"Yes, she has," he agreed. "I guess she was planning on working until Riley closed in a few years, but with the closing being moved up, she just doesn't want to make the move."

"How does your father feel about that?" Jamie asked.

Chris smiled. "Dad loves Mom so much that he would go along with anything that makes her happy."

Jamie's heart swelled. "You mean that he loves her so much that he only wants her to work if it makes her happy, not because she thinks that she has to?"

"That is exactly what I mean," he said as he pulled her close and began to kiss her.

Jamie had intended to bring up the subject of Annie to him that night, but as she felt herself melting into him, she decided to put it off for another day.

The next day was their final full day in Florida. As they walked along the beach that morning, they talked about what a perfect vacation it had been.

"I don't know how I am going to top this Christmas present next year," Chris laughed.

"Why don't we call the concert the Christmas present and the trip our honeymoon?" she offered. "And please don't think that you have to top that present. You are spoiling me."

"That is my absolute intention," he told her as he reached over and took her hand. "and if I ever stop, please let me know."

Jamie smiled. "There is something else that I want to talk to you about," she said.

"What is that?" he asked.

Jamie then told him about her conversation with her mother a few nights earlier. When she finished, she pointed out the comparison to the situation with Annie.

"I am really beginning to think that somehow she has learned the truth," Jamie said to him. "I know that it is not my place to initiate this, but I really think it's time to ...uh...put all the cards on the table. I'm concerned about her dealing with this alone."

Chris was quiet for a moment before he spoke. "I think that you may be right. I know that Granny said to give her space, but I don't want her to suffer needlessly if we can help her."

"It also occurred to me that someone has told her a story that is only partially true," Jamie said, "or possibly something that is worse than the truth."

"I hadn't considered that," he answered. "I think that when we get home and get settled, we need to have a talk with Mom and Dad."

"Will your mom put up a wall?" she asked.

"Possibly," he answered, "but I planned to be prepared."

"It is time," Jamie told him.

"Yes, it is," she agreed.

"While we are on the subject of parents, how do you feel about this situation with your mother and her old flame?"

Jamie thought for a moment. "I'm not sure. I'm still trying to process this whole story that she dropped on me." She looked over at him. "You know that I have a hard time dealing with unfaithfulness."

"I completely understand that," he told her. "It did sound like your father jumped ship first though,"

Jamie sighed. "I guess that part of growing up is realizing that your parents are fallible human beings who are as capable of messing up their lives as much as anyone else."

"That is very true," he answered. "I would suggest that you try to have an open mind about this guy tonight. Remember that he was not the one that your mother had the affair with."

"No, but he did leave her high and dry," she said.

"Yes, but that's between the two of them," he told her. "If being together makes them happy, then more power to them."

Jamie smiled. "How did I marry such a wise man?"

Chris laughed. "It is easy to be wise about other people's families. You haven't seen me figure out how to solve my family's problems have you?"

The four of them met at a popular seafood restaurant that had outside seating with a view of the ocean and a local marina, where some large yachts were coming and going. Jamie was pleasantly surprised to find that she liked Phil Jackson almost immediately. He was a tall man with brown hair that was speckled with flecks of grey, giving him a handsome distinguished look. He also had a warm welcoming smile. She also couldn't help but notice the way he looked at her mother. There seemed to be a connection there that she wanted to feel good about.

Phil immediately began to ask Chris questions about their farm and the cattle. Evidently, after his family moved to Colorado and he started college, his roommate was the son of a cattle rancher. He made several trips to the ranch and enjoyed the time that he spent there.

They also learned that Phil and his wife had never had any children, and Jamie suspected from the look in his eye that not having children was something that he deeply regretted.

After their dinner was over, they all walked down to the beach, and watched the sunset. It was a beautiful evening, and the show did not disappoint. When it was over, the group slowly walked back to the parking lot of the restaurant, where they talked for a few more minutes. Sharon invited the two of them to return in the summer after school was out and they invited her to visit them in Wisconsin during the hot month of August.

When Jamie said good-bye to her mother this time, she felt happier for her than she had in a long time. Since her father's death, both she and her mother had moved on with their lives and somehow, she knew that her father was at peace with the way things had worked out.

The next morning, Chris and Jamie arrived at the airport well ahead of time. As much as she hated leaving their condo and the beach, she was beginning to look forward to getting home and settling back into their lives. The following week, they had an appointment with a contractor to begin discussing plans for their new home.

Due to some thunderstorms that were in the area, their flight was delayed for two hours, so by the time that the plane finally took off, they were very anxious to arrive home.

Jamie slept most of the way home, so the flight passed quickly for her. Once they landed, it didn't take long to make their way to the baggage claim to collect their luggage. Shortly after that, they headed to the outside doors to catch a shuttle to long term parking.

When the doors opened, Jamie gasped. "Oh my, that air is cold, and I'm not sure but I think I just saw a snowflake!"

Chris laughed. "Welcome home."

A little over an hour later, they pulled into their driveway. Before he opened the truck door on his side, he leaned over and gave her a kiss. "That was an absolutely fantastic trip. I loved every minute of it, but I'm happy to be home with you, so we can start planning the rest of our lives."

"Ditto," she said as she kissed him back.

On the way to the front door, Chris called his mother.

"Hi," he said. "I just wanted to let you know that we are home."

"Oh Chris, I'm glad to know that." Her voice sounded frantic.

"Is something wrong?" he asked.

"Yes," she answered, nearly in tears. "I can't find Annie anywhere. I'm worried that she may have run away."

Chapter Fourteen

Ten minutes later, Chris and Jamie entered the living room of the Wilson home to find Jake and Mary both on their phones, obviously talking to people that they thought might have an idea where Annie could be. After a moment, they were both off the phone and Chris spoke.

"What the hell is going on?" he wanted to know.

Mary put her hand to her head and took a breath. "I went to school today to get some work done. I dropped her off at Angie's house before I went and her mother was going to bring her home around 3 because they were leaving to go to a family event in Madison, but when I got home at 4, she wasn't here. Jake was in town all afternoon, so she was here alone. I've been calling her phone and it keeps going straight to voicemail." Then she began to cry. "Dear God in heaven, I can't survive losing another child."

Jake stepped over to her and put his arms around her. "Mary, honey, you've got to calm down. There is no reason to think that we have lost her. The most likely explanation is that this is some kind of misunderstanding."

"Are you sure that Angie's mother dropped her off?" Chris asked.

Mary nodded. "I called her right away and she told me that they brought her here a little before three. She said that they stayed in the driveway until she was safely in the door."

"What makes you think that she may have run away?" Jamie wanted to know. "Did something happen?"

364

"I'm afraid so," Mary answered. "She and I had a terrible fight last night, and she was very unhappy with me."

"What did you fight about?" Jamie asked.

Mary hesitated and then spoke. "It was about Kyle's room. She started asking to move in there again. I told her no and then she got mad and told me how ridiculous it was to leave his room like that. Then she started sounding like Granny, saying how he either wouldn't or maybe even didn't like his room and all his things left like that."

Chris and Jamie exchanged a look. "Mom, you know she has a point. It's not fair to her," Chris said.

Mary gave her son a stern look. "This subject is not open for discussion."

"Mom…"

"Let's not argue about this right now," Jake said. "Let's find Annie and then we can worry about the room."

"Thank you for understanding," Mary said to her husband. "Unless you've gone through what we have, you can't understand."

Jamie could suddenly see that Mary was using guilt and grief to manipulate Jake into allowing her to protect the wall that she had carefully built around herself. After looking at Chris, she could see that he saw it too and he was not happy about it.

Jamie decided that maybe it was time to redirect the conversation to the subject of finding Annie. "Have you checked the barn?" she asked. "Is it possible that she went for a ride on her horse?"

"I did check the barn," Jake answered. "Her horse is in the stall exactly where it belongs."

"When you took her to Angie's, did she still seem upset about your argument?" Jamie asked.

Mary thought for a moment. "No, she was quiet, and I thought that she seemed a little tired, but she didn't seem as angry as she was last night. She said goodbye to me just as she usually did."

Suddenly, a thought came into Jamie's mind out of nowhere, and then she was certain that she knew where Annie was. It was very clear to her, and she couldn't believe that none of the other three of them had thought of it.

Something then told her to check for herself. "I'll be right back," she said and then headed for the stairs in the front room. Once she was upstairs, she walked quickly down the hall and opened the door to Kyle's room. When she flipped the light switch, the room flooded with light and she let out a sigh of relief to see Annie lying on his bed, sound asleep.

Jamie slowly walked over to the bed and sat down next to her. It only took a couple of gentle shakes for Annie to wake up. She sat up and looked at Jamie with a confused look.

"What are you doing here?" she asked.

Jamie smiled. "Chris and I just got home a little while ago. When he called your mother, she was quite upset because she had no idea where you were. She has been calling your phone, but it has been going straight to voicemail."

Annie reached over and picked her phone up from where it was lying on the bed. "I guess it is dead," she told Jamie. "I forgot to put it on the charger last night."

"Did you come in here for some reason and then fall asleep on this bed?" Jamie asked. Annie nodded without saying anything.

Jamie thought for a moment and then asked her another question. "Do you come in here a lot?"

Annie nodded again. "Whenever I come in here, I feel good. It's as if I'm close to ...Kyle."

After staring at the child for a moment, she spoke again. "Annie, honey, is there something that you would like to tell your mother...and the rest of us?"

The girl stared at her as if she was undecided about what to say. "I think that you...and everyone else would feel better if you were completely honest," Jamie told her. "Come on. I'll be right there with you."

After a moment, Annie gave a slight nod and then Jamie stood up and held out her hand. Then the two of them walked down the stairs together.

When Mary saw Annie, she ran to her and pulled her into a hug. She held onto her for a moment and then she let go and a confused look came across her face.

"Where were you?" she asked. "I checked your room several times."

Annie's face seemed to pale and then she spoke quietly. "I was laying on Kyle's bed and I guess I fell asleep. I forgot to charge my phone last night, so I guess it died. I'm sorry. I didn't mean to worry you."

"I don't want to start this argument again, but what were you doing in Kyle's room?" Mary asked. "You know that I want it left alone."

"I think maybe Annie has something that she wants to tell us," Jamie said.

"If this is about moving the rooms, we have been over all this," Mary answered.

This time Chris interjected. "Mom, I have a feeling that this is something more than that," he said.

"But..." Mary tried to say.

"Let's all sit down and listen to Annie," Jake said in a tone that made it clear that the decision was final.

When they were all seated, Chris looked at Annie and said, "Go ahead. We are all listening."

Annie took a deep breath and then began. "I don't know exactly when I started going in

Kyle's room. Chris has always told me what a great big brother he was, so I would go in there and being in there always made me feel good, like he was watching over me, and that he understood whatever I was going through. You know, like he was being a big brother to me.

That was great, but after a while, I started feeling like there was something I was missing. Eventually, I got this feeling that I was supposed to look for something, so I started poking around through his drawers."

At that point, Jamie thought she heard a small gasp come from Mary. Annie suddenly was quiet, so Chris tried to help her along.

"Did you find anything important?" he asked.

Annie nodded. "I found a copy of my birth certificate," she said in a quiet voice.

"Dear God," Mary said in a near whisper as she covered her face with her hands.

"Yes, Mom. I know the truth," Annie said. "I know that Kyle was my father and Holly Gibson was my mother."

There was a deafening silence in the room at that point. Then Annie, who seemed relieved to be unloading her burdens, dropped another big piece of news on them. "I also found the court order giving him custody of me and the paper that she signed giving up all of her rights to me." She paused for a moment and then continued. "She was not a nice person."

"Did you somehow find out that she was a cheerleader?" Jamie wanted to know.

Annie nodded." I found some of Kyle's year books and I went through them."

"And this is the reason behind your extreme dislike of cheerleaders?" Jamie wanted to know.

A single tear flowed down Annie's cheek as she nodded again. "She was all about cheering and looking pretty, but she didn't care at all about her own daughter."

The room was quiet again for another moment and then Jake spoke. "Sweetheart, she was very young, and I think that she was very frightened to become a mother at such a young age."

Jamie stole a glance at Mary. Her face was pale, and she was sitting quietly absorbing all the conversation. Annie's next statement was another total surprise.

"Did you know that after she moved away, she tried to convince my father to leave me here with you and come to live with her in California?"

Mary suddenly came to life. It was obvious that this was news to her. "Where did you get information like that?" Then her eyes narrowed. "Is that some nonsense that Granny told you?"

"No," Annie replied. "I went through his phone that is on his dresser. His charger was still plugged into the wall, so I charged it and then I read all his text messages. It was just a few days before...the accident."

Jake and Mary looked at each other. "That explained why he seemed upset toward the end," Jake said.

Mary nodded. "Yes, I remember having a discussion with you about what might have been bothering him."

"What did he say to her?" Chris wanted to know.

"He told her that there was no way he would do that," she said. "Then he sent her a bunch of pictures of me and told her how much he loved me. She didn't respond. A few minutes later, he begged her to come back so that they could raise me together."

"Did she respond to that at all?" Jake asked.

"Not until the next day," Annie replied. "She said that she just couldn't do it, because she had her life planned and a baby just didn't fit into it. She went on to say that he was welcome to be a part of her life, as long as it didn't include me."

"Oh, my poor Kyle," Mary said, and then she stood and walked over to the desk in the corner to get some tissues.

"Mom," Annie said. "I know that you have a hard time believing in the things that Granny used to talk about, but I need you to listen to something else and kind of keep an open mind."

Mary took a deep breath and said, "All right. Let's get it all out."

"What I am about to say didn't come from Granny," she began. "We never talked about this. These are all things I have felt and figured out for myself. First, I felt like my father, Kyle, was with me in his room. I never saw him in the room or heard his voice; I just felt him there. I think that is why I kept going back to the room. He wanted me there because he wanted me to learn the truth." After a moment, she asked, "You all don't think I'm crazy, do you?"

"No," Chris quickly responded. "There have been times when I've been working in the barn alone, and he has suddenly popped into my mind, and I have wondered if he was there with me."

Jake added his own reassurance. "The same thing has happened to me."

"Do you think that he is here now?" Mary asked in a quiet, but possibly hopeful voice.

Annie shook her head. "No," she answered in a sad voice. "He left with Granny."

"With Granny?" Mary asked, somewhat confused.

Annie turned to Jamie. "Do you remember the day of Granny's funeral and I asked you if you saw it?"

Jamie nodded. "I thought that you were asking me if I saw the deer up on the hill, which I did. I thought it was odd that a deer would stand that close to a large group of people, but I have a feeling that you saw something more than that."

Annie nodded slowly. "Granny and Kyle were standing behind the deer, and they were both waving good-bye. I felt sad that they would leave but then this warm feeling came over me like everything was going to be all right. I don't know why, but for some reason I felt like I should look at you. When I did, I knew that you had seen something too. Then the minister started to pray, and when he was finished, I looked back at the hill and there was nothing there."

"Dear God in heaven," Mary said. "It makes sense now."

"What?" Annie asked.

"The night after the funeral, I had a strange dream," she said. "I marked it off as a reaction to Granny's death. Now I see that it was more than that."

"Tell us about it," Chris said.

"I saw Granny and Kyle together," she told them. "They waved at me, and Kyle said, 'It's time'. I thought that he was telling me that it was time for him to move on."

"Or maybe he meant that it is time for all of us to move on," Chris said, looking directly at his mother.

Mary looked at her son, and the two of them exchanged a long look. "You are right," she told him. Then she looked at Annie. "You can have Kyle's room."

Tears rolled down Annie's cheeks. "Thank you, Mom. I know that this isn't easy for you."

"I would just like to ask one thing," Mary replied.

"What's that?" Annie asked.

"I would like for your father...Jake, and I to go through the room alone and pick out some things that we would like to keep. Then you and your brother can go through it and choose what you want to keep and get rid of everything else."

"When all of that is done, could we paint the walls a brighter color and get a new bedspread and curtains?" Annie wanted to know.

"I think that is a wonderful idea," Mary answered. "We'll do it together."

Annie then moved over next to her mother and the two of them exchanged a long hug. A moment later, Annie looked at Jamie and Chris. "There is one thing that I would like to have for my new room. It's something of yours."

"What is that?" Chris asked.

"Could I possibly have the rocking chair?" she wanted to know. "Barney would love to have that in my room and maybe he would stop running to your house. We found him over there four or five times, during the last week. And since the chair seems to be open to *"visitors from the other side"*, maybe, just maybe, my father or Granny might drop by from time to time to have a rock."

"That is a great idea," Jamie told her. Then she giggled. "I think that it has served its purpose for me. The chair and its antics annoy Chris anyway."

"Yes," Chris answered. "Please come and get the damn thing anytime that you want."

They all laughed at his response and suddenly there was a lighthearted happiness that filled the home. It was as if everyone and everything had settled into their rightful place.

Epilogue

Five Years Later

    Jamie stood back and looked at her work. The back porch was covered with balloons that had Annie's graduation picture on them. There were two decorated tables set up on one wall. One was for food and the other was for gifts. There was another table covered with memorabilia of Annie's high school days on the adjacent wall. Out in the yard, there were several more tables set up for guests to enjoy the catered food that would arrive later.

Jamie took one last look at the display table. She smiled as she saw the picture of Kyle at one side of it. That had been Annie's idea because she wanted her father to be a part of this important day in her life.

In the years since that impactful night after she and Chris had returned from their honeymoon, all their lives had changed. Mary had let go of her wall of grief and she and Annie had grown closer. The two of them worked together to create Annie's dream room in Kyle's old bedroom. Jamie had helped out by sewing the curtains and helping to make a memory board about her father to hang in the room.

Mary decided that Annie needed some help working through her anger about her mother, so she took her to a therapist. The sessions seemed to help because eventually, she let go of her anger towards all girls who were cheerleaders, and she was able to resume her friendship with Lacey. Her high school years were happy, and she spent lots of time with friends. During her senior year, she dated a boy that all the family liked. After graduation, she planned to go to a fashion design school in Milwaukee.

Chris and Jamie were able to get their new house built at the end of the first summer of their marriage. In July of that year, Bessie did decide to retire, and Jamie was offered Bessie's position at the Valene School. However, at about that same time, she discovered that she was pregnant. After some discussion, she and Chris decided that she would stay home and take care of the baby. Two years later, she became pregnant again, so she further delayed her return to teaching. She found that she loved being a stay-at-home mother. Nora, who was now four years old, was a very busy inquisitive child. She was always full of questions, and she seemed to never run out of ideas of things to do. Jacob was now almost two years old, and he was full of energy. Jamie's days were full, and she always went to bed tired, but it was a good tired.

Chris was able to put together the original farm that was listed from the 19th century. His days were also long and busy, but he was mostly working in a supervisory duty. All the land was either used for cattle or was cash rented. It was a good life for both of them.

To Jamie's surprise, Leslie also decided not to make the move to the Valene School. She and Joe were married the following September. They also started a family immediately, and she and Jamie often arranged play dates for their children.

Eddie received a promotion from his firm and moved to Chicago. He and Sara continued a long-distance relationship for nearly a year. Then her father died, and she and her mother moved to the city and the last that Jamie heard was that she had placed her mother in a senior living home and she and Eddie were making wedding plans.

"Annie will be pleased when she returns from shopping with Lacey," Mary said as she stepped out the door. "The display table looks really nice."

Mary stood quietly looking at the table for a moment and Jamie could almost read her mind. "Annie is handling her mother's most recent rejection well, isn't she?"

After sighing, Mary answered her. "Yes, she is handling it better than I would have."

A few years earlier, Annie admitted that she had been searching for her biological mother for some time, and that she had finally located her on

Facebook. Holly was living in Modesto California. She was a divorced mother of three children. Annie had been looking at her Facebook page since then, but now that she was graduating from high school, she decided that the time had come to reach out to her. Jake and Mary had a long talk with her, and they told her that it was her decision, but they wanted her to understand the risks that were involved.

Annie gave it some thought, and then she sent her a heartfelt message explaining who she was and what was going on in her life. Mary had a couple of sleepless nights worrying that Holly would have the same reaction to Annie that she had had to them when they let her know that Kyle had died.

Evidently, Holly had grown up some over the years because her response was polite, but somewhat distant. She congratulated her on her accomplishments and wished her well in her future endeavors, but she didn't offer any possibility of any further connection. Annie seemed to take the lukewarm brush off in stride. If it upset her, she didn't let it show.

Jamie looked at her watch. "Oh, look at the time," she said. "I need to get home. I'm sure that

Jacob is up from his nap by now and between the two of them, Chris is probably running circles around himself."

Mary laughed. "Give my grandbabies a kiss for me," she said. "We will see you here later."

"All right," Jamie said. She then walked to her car and began the short drive home. Just as she was about to pull out of the driveway, she saw a UPS truck turning onto Ranch Road. "I hope that he is bringing the new blinds that I ordered for Nora's room," she said to herself.

A few minutes later, she found Chris alone in the kitchen, apparently cleaning up from the snack that he had just given the kids. "What did you do with the children?" she asked him.

"They are in the family room watching the Lion King," he told her. "I just checked on them and they are both completely in the zone."

"Well, I'm happy to hear that all is well," she answered. "I think that the porch is all set up and ready for the party."

"Good," he said. "Have you heard from Phil and your mom?"

"Yes," she told him. "Their plane landed about 11:30, and they have checked into their hotel. Mom said that they would be at the party around 6."

"Great," he answered and then he walked over to her and put his arms around her. "Our life is good, isn't it?"

"I would say that it is just about perfect," she said just before he began to kiss her.

A few hours later, there was a nice crowd of people on the Wilson's porch and in their backyard. Nora and Jacob were playing with Joe and Leslie's two children on the playset that Jake and Chris had built the summer before. Chris and Joe were keeping an eye on them because Jamie was helping Mary with the food, and Leslie was sitting in a nearby lawn chair, because their latest arrival was due any day and the doctor had ordered her to take it easy. Jamie placed a fresh bowl of salad on the food table and looked over at her friend. She smiled because she knew that she and Chris were keeping a secret. This, however, was Annie's day and the news of their next addition to the family could wait.

Annie stood near her display table greeting guests. She seemed to be enjoying all the attention. Her boyfriend, Kevin, stayed fairly close by her side. He was planning to attend college in Chicago, hoping to become an engineer. The two of them seemed to have a practical attitude about their relationship. They both seemed to understand the importance of continuing their education, and they acknowledged that long-distance relationships could be difficult, but they were planning to just take things as they came.

Several hours later, the guests were gone, and the family was gathered in the living room. Annie was opening the gifts and envelopes that had been left at the party. When she was about halfway through, she noticed a small brown box lying in the middle of all the cards.

"What's that?" she asked, pointing at the box.

"The UPS man brought that this afternoon," Mary told her.

The strange Granny like look that Annie sometimes still got, came across her face. Then after a moment, she reached out and picked up the box. Once it was open, she found a card and another small box. She opened the card first and when she read the words, tears came to her eyes.

"Annie,

I just want you to know that I am very proud of you. It would seem that you have grown into a very fine young woman. Jake and Mary have done a wonderful job raising you; probably better than I could have ever done. Inside the small box is a necklace that your father gave to me on my 18th birthday. I want you to have it. I'm sure that wherever he is, he is proud of you too. Good luck with school next year. Let me know how you are doing.

Holly"

"It's from my...bio...mother," Annie explained to the rest of them and then read the message out loud. Then she opened the small box and pulled out a silver necklace with a heart-shaped pendant.

Mary gasped. "I remember that necklace," she said. "Kyle was so excited about giving that to her for her birthday. It was just before they found out..."

"About me?" Annie asked, and Mary nodded.

"I'll be right back," Annie said and then she suddenly jumped up and ran upstairs. She returned a few short minutes later, with a picture in her hand. It was a photo of Kyle and Holly, and the necklace was displayed clearly.

Mary smiled. "That picture was taken the night he took her out for her birthday dinner," she said. "It was the same night that he gave her the necklace." She was quiet for a moment and then continued. "That was a wonderful gift for her to give you."

"Yes," Annie answered. "It was." Then she slipped the necklace over her head. After a moment, she asked Mary a question. "There was a time when they were happy, wasn't there?"

Mary smiled. "Yes, they were happy, and I'm sure that both of them want you to be happy too."

"I am," Annie said with a smile. "Tonight, I am very happy."

Upstairs, the rocking chair began to slowly peacefully rock.

Books by Debbie Williams

Romantic Suspense Titles

Daring to Hope - 2013

Daring to Love – The Sequel to Daring to Hope - 2014

Rocky Mountain Way - 2015

Living and Loving in Arizona Series

Tara's Legend – 2016

Sarah's Family – 2017

Friends in the Fold – 2017

Living in the Fold – 2018

Weddings and Funerals -2018

Ryan's Daughters – 2019

Kevin's Wish – A Christmas Novella - 2019

The Accident – 2022

Embracing Change - 2023

Historical Fiction Titles

Losing Warren -2020

Picturing the Past – The Sequel to Losing Warren - 2020

Unsettled Waters – A Romantic Tale of Wartime Intrigue 2021

Hillsboro's Mystery Child – The Story of Sarah Dorney Stroup 2021

For the Love of Fallsville – A Highland County Ghost Town – 2022

Paranormal Tales

Kate's Journey – A Paranormal Tale – 2015

With Love from Sandy – A Paranormal Novella – 2020

Made in the USA
Columbia, SC
25 August 2023

22052075R00213